OBSESSED HOPE

A SLAYING LOVE NOVEL
BOOK 6

AMANDA SIEGRIST

McCord Family Novel

Protecting You

Trust in Love

Deserving You

Always Kind of Love

Finding You

Dare You to Love

Mona & Mason

The Paranormal Chronicles, Volume 1

Perfect For You Novel

The Wrong Brother

The Right Time

The Easy Part

The Hard Choice

Psychic Love Novel

Exploding Love

Captured Love

Slaying Love Novel

Won't Let You Go

Doomed Love

Deadly Crazy

Evidence of Sin

Finding Redemption

Obsessed Hope

A QUICK NOTE...

You will see from chapters 1-5 writing prompts at the very beginning. I love writing flash fiction. I haven't done it in quite awhile, but every Friday I used to write a new scene with prompts given to me by my lovely readers in my reader group. These prompts are from that. That's how some of my stories are born. When I was asked to be in the *Out of the Shadows charity anthology*, I decided to resurrect (lol that sounds so intense) my ONE TASTE SERIES. Based on the few scenes I had written, I thought they'd fit perfectly with the other characters, and they do! At least, I think so. I *hope* you think so, too. Thank you for your support—always! THIS BOOK WAS PREVIOUSLY A PART OF THE OUT OF THE SHADOWS ANTHOLOGY.

HAPPY READING!
💜 MUCH LOVE, AMANDA SIEGRIST

A DETECTIVE WITH LETHAL INSTINCTS. A WOMAN WHO ATTRACTS DANGER. AN OBSESSION THAT COULD DESTROY THEM BOTH.

1

WRITING PROMPT ~ RUN.

"Why do I feel like this happens way too often?"

"Probably because it has lately."

"It's annoying as hell."

"Says the man who always insists on rock, paper, scissors when it does happen."

Rory rolled his eyes at his partner, Reese, refusing to acknowledge that. Just because two sets of detectives showed up at a crime scene, it didn't mean he wasn't going to argue about the fact. They showed up first, so therefore, it was their case. End of discussion. What annoyed him the most was their new captain seemed to be an idiot, continuing to do shit like this.

"Well, well, well. What do we have here?" Detective Zeke Chance asked with a little too much cheeriness for Rory's sake. It was barely seven a.m. Why did he have to look so chipper? Not to mention, they were at the scene of a dead body.

"Us, at our crime scene. We showed up first," Rory spit out without preamble, then took a sip of his coffee.

"By like five minutes, if that. Have you even looked at the scene yet?" Detective Ben Stoyer, Zeke's partner in crime and best friend, replied.

"Dr. Everly told us to wait out here until he had a look with Susan," Reese replied as if they weren't about to fight over who got dibs on this case.

"Which implies we were here first and it's our case," Rory said, trying for the same upbeat attitude as Zeke had.

"The captain called us," Zeke said.

"He called us, too." Which was why Rory was annoyed. Why couldn't the man get it together? Call one set of detectives for a case and leave it at that. Sometimes, it felt like the man was trying to create conflict in the workplace.

"I always lose at rock, paper, scissors." Ben shrugged. "Even to my niece Isabella. You do it this time."

"You're as bad as Rory," Reese said with a chuckle. Then he grabbed the coffee out of Rory's hands and took a large sip.

Always taking his stuff, like he had the right. Just because they were partners—and best friends—didn't mean he wanted to share his shit with him, especially his coffee. It was way too early to be dealing with this bullshit.

Yet, he didn't argue, especially when Zeke eyed the exchange, a slight twinkle in his eyes. Reese took another sip, then handed it back to Rory. *Note to self, don't forget Reese's coffee next time.* He usually brought him a cup as well, but he had a rough night sleeping after dealing with his ex again. Then the captain called, waking him out of a decent sleep he had finally managed to get.

"Come on, Ben, let's show them how it's done." Reese put up his hands, one fist over his palm.

Zeke chuckled as Ben mimicked Reese's hand gesture.

Rock, paper, scissors was always his go-to growing up

with two brothers. Fights started so easily, even over something as simple as who got to use the bathroom first. He was an expert at it, and he normally won.

He taught his partner well when Ben lost the game getting his rock covered by Reese's paper.

"See, I never win," Ben grumbled.

"Better luck next time." Rory winked and then headed for the house.

He waited long enough for Dr. Everly. Reese joined him shortly after saying good-bye to Zeke and Ben, who he knew no doubt would find another case soon enough. Or hell, keep working on one of their open cases.

The dead man, Mr. Fontain, was found in bed, arms outstretched and tied to the bedposts, naked, strangled with a tie. By the looks of it, in the throes of passion, if the condom still wrapped around his dick was any indication.

Sex games gone too far? Revenge murder? Had one woman on the side and his current woman didn't appreciate that?

The housekeeper called it in. According to her, he wasn't married, no girlfriend that she knew of.

"Well?" Rory took a sip of coffee as he continued to glance around the room. Nothing looked disturbed, as if whoever had killed him hadn't rummaged through his drawers. Not a robbery.

"Always the conversationalist, Detective Walker," Dr. Everly said dryly, then leaned away from the bed where he was inspecting the man's neck. Yeah, Rory didn't have much patience—especially in the mornings when he was woken up too early—or tact when it came to pretty much everything. Probably why Dr. Everly wanted him to wait outside while he did his preliminary check on the body. Rory tended to get on his nerves more often than not.

"He appears to be have been strangled by the tie. We'll see if the autopsy confirms."

"You don't think so?" Reese asked.

"It appears so, but like I said, I want to confirm when I do the autopsy. It feels..." Dr. Everly shrugged. "Staged in a way. I don't know why. Although, there are red marks around his wrists as if he struggled. I imagine he did if he was strangled by the tie."

Susan cleared her throat. "Or you don't think a woman could have done this."

"I didn't say that." Dr. Everly pushed up his glasses and offered Susan a gentle smile as if trying to apologize for whatever he might've been insinuating.

"Well, condom, naked, tied to the bed, a tie around his neck. All signs he was having some kinky sex when he died," Reese said. "Makes sense it would be a woman. She starts squeezing harder than he anticipates with the tie, and although she might be smaller, she's got the upper hand. He's tied up. He's not going anywhere. He's dead within less than a minute."

"All true. I always like to perform an autopsy before confirming," Dr. Everly replied.

"I did a small cursory glance when I got here. No signs of forced entry. Lola, the housekeeper, said she unlocked the front door. Whoever was here, Roger Fontain knew them. Let them in, and they locked the door on their way out. Either stole a key—because she said the deadlock was set— or had a key of their own."

"Time of death?" Rory asked.

"A simple please and thank you would go a long way, detective," Dr. Everly said tersely.

Okay, Rory's tone of voice was a bit too clipped this morning. Hello, not a morning person. He couldn't help it.

He produced a friendly smile. The last thing he wanted to do was upset Dr. Everly. The man held all the answers he'd need to solve this case. "Please."

"Based on the rigor mortis of the body, I'd say somewhere between midnight and three a.m."

"Thanks, doc," Rory replied.

"Dr. Everly." The usually friendly coroner was quick to correct him—with a stern tone.

Rory couldn't hold back the chuckle. He knew Dr. Everly didn't like to be called doc, but sometimes it was fun to needle the guy.

Even Susan chuckled. Reese had the good sense to stay quiet when Dr. Everly glared at the two of them.

"Let us know if you find something good." Rory looked at Susan as he said it, and added a grin, but nothing too flirty. Susan's husband might not be here, but Stitch was a man who didn't stand for anyone flirting with his wife, even if it was in friendliness. The last thing he wanted to do was get on her husband's bad side. Not a dude to mess with. He knew Sauer had gotten into it with Stitch one time and he didn't walk away without a scratch. Although, Sauer had held his own.

Susan nodded and returned a smile.

"He works at an advertising company or something. Let's canvas the neighborhood, then hit up his place of employment." Reese walked out first.

Sounded like a solid plan.

They walked around the house before leaving. Mr. Fontain had nice tastes. Expensive paintings on the wall. Good china in the cupboards. A wine collection worthy of wanting to stash a few bottles under his coat. He made good money at his job.

Talking to the neighbors—most were still home, since it

was so early in the morning—yielded nothing. Why would they have seen anything? Everyone had been asleep at that time of night. No one had seen anyone visit Mr. Fontain before night fell either.

When they arrived at his place of employment and asked to speak to his secretary, Rory felt the first giddy feeling of the day.

She wasn't here. Called in sick.

Left early yesterday as well. Mr. Fontain had left shortly after her.

They had also argued, yet no one knew why.

Finally, a lead.

Maybe to their killer.

"YOU KNOW WHAT, don't look at me that way." She cocked a brow. "You're so damn judgmental."

Brooke grabbed another mini powdered doughnut, chomping with emphasis as she stared at her annoying cat, Willow. She was a beautiful black-and-white tuxedo cat, but with so much sassiness, she thought she ruled the house. Which wasn't too far off when Brooke thought about it.

She wanted to be fed? Meowed and meowed until Brooke stopped whatever she was doing—sleep included—to stop the incessant noise.

She insisted on being petted? Nudged her furry face into her hands until Brooke gave her soft, little rubs under her neck. Her favorite spot.

Snack time? Yep. More meowing until she got her way.

Willow ruled the house, and Brooke honestly wouldn't change a thing. Because when she needed comfort, Willow was there. When she needed company, Willow to the rescue.

When she needed to vent about her tyrant boss—asshole with grabby hands—Willow always delivered the best disgusted looks, like she couldn't believe the nerve the jackass had. When her latest boyfriend turned out to be a loser, Willow to the rescue with cuddles.

She could always count on Willow to be there for her. Reliable and steady.

Something she couldn't say about anyone else in her life. How sad.

Hell, she could even rely on Willow to judge her as she ate another doughnut—number five, to be exact. She was supposed to be on a diet. Something she tried every other month and always failed. No matter how many times Willow glared at her with her beady, green eyes, she always grabbed one more handful of whatever snack she had caved in and bought.

What could she say? She loved food. Food loved her. She didn't even know why she attempted to diet; it never worked.

Meow.

Brooke rolled her eyes and snatched her hand away from the bag of doughnuts. "Fine. I'll stop. Quit with your hollering."

Meow.

Then her tail flowed back and forth as she turned around and walked away. Of course with her head held high as if she were showing off her crown.

Brooke eyed the bag, then huffed with annoyance and walked away. She should've never bought the bag in the first place because she could devour a bag in one day all on her own. But it had been so tempting when she stopped at the store last night after work for milk, bread, and eggs. After shoving her boss away from another attempt of getting in her pants, she had wanted to drown her sorrows in something. Since she didn't drink often—alcohol tasted nasty to her, except for a nice crisp glass of white wine—she chose junk food as her poor-pity-me comfort food. Ice cream was so cliché. Doughnuts were more her choice of woe-is-me.

She should go to human resources about his behavior. But she couldn't afford to lose her job, and he had threatened to fire her on numerous occasions.

The bastard.

She needed more of a backbone. She needed to stand up for herself.

Tomorrow.

Tomorrow would be the day she'd go to human resources and file an official complaint against him.

Today she planned to eat a few more doughnuts—hey, she couldn't let it go to waste—and enjoy her hooky day. She had called in sick, needing a day to herself. To get her emotions back in place—and to avoid her boss for at least one day.

Everyone deserved a hooky day, and she hadn't taken one in—well, never. She always played things by the book. Followed the rules. Didn't speed—something that drove her last boyfriend up the wall. He never let her drive after the one time he found her following the speed limit to the number. It said thirty-five miles per hour, she went thirty-five miles per hour. Not to mention, he was a bit of a control freak and argued when she insisted on driving—just the one time. They were living in the twenty-first century; women driving for a date wasn't unusual. At least, it shouldn't be, in Brooke's eyes.

Life was exhausting lately.

Asshole boss.

Controlling ex-boyfriend, who couldn't get a clue they were done.

She had needed a day to herself, and for once, she decided to take it.

Heading to her room to change into shorts, she saw Willow sitting on the bed, eyeing her with her judgy eyes still.

Waving her shorts in front of her, she laughed. "See. Going for a run, like I said I would. Stop getting on my case about it."

Willow circled once on the bed, then laid down completely, stretching out her body in a languid move.

"You just have to rub it in. When I'm done running, I'm going to curl up under the blankets and take a nap, too. So there."

She changed and put on her running shoes, ruffled Willow's head, which the silly cat pushed into her hand looking for more, then walked out of the room with a smile.

She could always count on Willow to brighten her mood, even with her sassy attitude and demanding ways.

Locking the door on her way out, she jogged in place on her porch, trying to get herself in the mood. She wasn't a huge fan of running, but she also didn't like going to the gym. Too many people. Too many eyes on her. No, thanks.

Not to mention, that's where she met her latest why-did-I-even-date-you boyfriend. If she wanted to go back to the gym, she'd have to find a new one. There was no way she wanted to run into Ted for any reason, especially since he didn't understand the words 'we're done.'

"You got this, Brooke. You can do it."

Yeah, she talked to herself too much. She should stop that.

"Run!"

But today wouldn't be the day she did. With her pep talk done, she jaunted off the porch and headed toward the same route she always did. A quick run around the block. A simple circle. It took her about fifteen minutes, and she was always sweating and breathing heavily at the end. But it always made her feel more energized. Running sucked in the moment, but it was always worth it in the end.

She cleared her head of all negative thoughts as she ran. Focused on putting one foot in front of the other. By the time she turned the last corner and headed back toward her house, she was out of breath and dripping with sweat. As usual.

As she neared her driveway, she slowed down, eyeing the unknown vehicle parked and the man standing by it.

He was dressed in a gray suit, his tie loose around his neck. Classic brown hair, a bit longer and swooped back with perfection she would've failed to master. A day's growth beard, maybe a few days, filled his cheeks, although she could see the sharp jawline. One she'd describe as kissable. Not that she daydreamed about guys' kissable jawlines.

What an odd thought.

Even Ted hadn't had a kissable jawline. And the bedroom techniques, well, he kind of sucked in that department, too. Not that she let him get all the way in her pants. She hadn't felt the connection, so she held him off.

This man looked like he knew all the right moves.

Get a grip, Brooke.

Shaking off naughty thoughts, she ran toward him instead of her front door.

He wore sunglasses that shielded his eyes, which bothered her for some reason. She wanted to see his eyes. Because with the fierce frown on his face, this wouldn't be a happy visit.

Geez, what had she done? Nothing. Minding her own business on her hooky day.

The closer she got, she realized he had a bit of gray hair sprinkled on the sides, close-shaven, probably making it easier to comb his hair back as he did. A bit of gray on his chin as well.

A sexy silver fox if she ever saw one.

Mind, get out of gutter.

She stopped in front of him, breathing heavily, embarrassed by her appearance. Sweat dripped down her face. Glistening chest. Probably didn't smell too pleasant either. Well, whatever, she wasn't out to impress anyone. Just get her workout in for the day.

"Can I help you?"

"You don't appear sick."

Odd thing to say.

"I'm sorry?"

The man removed his glasses, his green eyes piercing her with a look that made her want to drop to her knees in pain. Cat-like eyes that held a world of judgment, like Willow.

"You called out of work today. You don't appear sick."

Wow. Her boss was—ugh! She couldn't even find the right word for that asshole. But enough was enough. She refused to let that jackass get his way all the time. Control her life and think he was untouchable.

Her eyes narrowed. "Who are you?"

His hand went to his jacket where he pulled it away from his chest—super muscular, if she had to guess—and flashed a badge clipped to his belt and a gun close by it.

"Detective Rory Walker. Your boss was found murdered this morning. Where were you between the hours of midnight and three a.m.?"

Her jaw dropped, and her entire body nearly dropped to the ground. But she managed to hold herself together and stay upright. She could feel her heart pounding, but this time not from the run she just endured.

No. Nope. She had to have misheard him. Her boss couldn't be dead. He was too stubborn of an asshole to do something like that.

"Ms. Duncan?"

Right. Mr. Sexy with an attitude wasn't lying to her about her boss. And he didn't seem to have any patience either.

Men. Such ridiculous creatures.

"Home."

"Can anyone verify that?"

Her asshole boss...dead.

She still couldn't believe it.

"Ms. Duncan? I asked you a question."

Ugh. From one asshole to the next. All men were the same. Yet, this man seemed very...well, suspicious of her. Like she had killed her boss. How ridiculous. She barely escaped his clutches last night in his office.

"Yes. I was home all night with Willow."

Oops. Wrong thing to say. Willow was her cat. Not exactly the best witness to verify her alibi. But it was true. She *was* at home all night with Willow.

"I'll need to speak to her."

But it had been a helluva day yesterday, and today obviously wasn't going to go much better. Small laughter slipped out before she could stop herself.

"Sure. Follow me. She's inside the house."

Boy, he was in for a rude awakening. He deserved it for his abrupt manner. She didn't kill anyone. How dare he think so.

She walked away toward her front door, knowing exactly the kind of greeting Willow would give Detective Walker.

Hisses and claws galore. She wasn't a huge people person, especially with men.

Just one of the many reasons she broke up with Ted. Willow didn't like him.

And anyone Willow didn't like wasn't worth her time.

2

WRITING PROMPT ~ NOT GOOD ENOUGH. YOUR CAT ATTACKED ME. SERIOUSLY.

RORY FOLLOWED the woman toward her house, wondering how long this would take. It didn't take a genius to figure out this woman didn't kill her boss. Roger Fontain had been strangled with a tie. This woman looked like it killed her to run around the block. He had seen her run out of her house and followed her a bit before driving back to her house to wait for her. The strength it would take to hold a man down and strangle him wasn't something he thought this woman was capable of. Even with the evidence that Mr. Fontain had been tied to the bed and couldn't fight back.

Not to mention, a small, teeny-tiny part of him didn't like to think about her on top of someone disgusting like Mr. Fontain. He wasn't old and fat, but he had a small pudge on him. Not someone he'd considered handsome either, not that he had a thing for guys. But if he did, Mr. Fontain wouldn't even rate a one out of ten.

This woman—Brooke Duncan—was beautiful, even with sweat rolling down her cheek. A cute kind of beautiful. Sandy-brown hair pulled into a loose ponytail. Amber-golden eyes that looked at him as if she wanted to spit at him. Not surprising, since he had had an accusatory tone with her. And a sweet, adorable smile that had been hard to look away from. He had never seen anyone smile as they ran. He hated running. And okay, it wasn't hard to notice the lovely set of breasts she had. They were held in with a good sports bra, but they still jiggled as she ran, and it had been very difficult to look away. They would fit perfectly in his hands.

Which was something he needed to get out of his head right this second. He was working a case, not here to ogle a woman who he didn't think would even hurt a fly.

He'd do his job like he always did and eliminate her as a suspect with actual evidence and not the way his gut always told him what was up. The new captain never liked it when he said his gut told him so. Seriously. The thing spoke up all the time. What else could he say? He liked to say his 'gut told him so' a lot, but only because it annoyed Captain Johnson. Since the guy never made any of their lives easy, he figured it was his duty to get on his nerves. He sure missed Captain Ganderson, but he understood the guy wanted to retire and travel around the world with his wife.

Maybe if Rory's marriage wouldn't have ended so badly, he would've wanted to sightsee with her as well.

Ms. Duncan unlocked her door and stepped inside, grasping the side of the door as he walked in as well. He didn't miss the way her knuckles looked white, her hand shaking.

So she was nervous. Interesting. He didn't think she killed her boss, but what could she be nervous about?

But his gut could be wrong. It had never happened before, but he also never thought his wife would cheat on him with the neighbor, so there was that.

Next time Reese wanted to split up and tackle different

things on the case, he'd tell him no. If this woman did kill her boss, he had just stepped into the den alone, with no backup. Maybe she was one of those femme fatale types. Lured men in, then struck without notice, bringing them down without them even blinking.

And maybe he watched too much late-night TV trying to fall asleep and forget the bad memories of his life.

Or maybe she was nervous because he wasn't exactly a people person. He came off abrupt to...well, everyone. But it's one of the reasons he liked homicide. Dead people didn't talk back. And when it came to solving a crime, he didn't care how he came off to anyone because his main goal was to catch the bad guy. Dealing with actual victims always twisted his stomach the wrong way. Literally to the point he wanted to puke. He couldn't handle their emotions. Too high-strung. Too chaotic. Too emotional. Too many tears. Too much anger. He always left the victims and the deceased loves ones to Reese. He was much better with them.

So, yeah, he loved homicide. His dead victims never gave him problems.

She closed the door and gave him a weak smile.

"Willow, your alibi? Where is she?"

Her smile wavered.

Great. She was lying to him. There was no Willow. Which meant she didn't have a solid alibi. For some odd reason, it bugged him. He couldn't pinpoint exactly why, but it did.

Probably because he wanted in her pants because she had a nice ass and a good rack on her. Running outfits were his new favorite.

"Oh, there you are, Willow. Come say hi to Detective Walker."

Rory followed her gaze toward the hallway near a set of stairs that led up to the second level. A black-and-white cat strolled closer, its tail wagging leisurely.

This was a joke.

It had to be.

He pulled his attention away from the cat, who didn't come too close—which made him happy—and looked at Ms. Duncan.

"Where's Willow?"

He'd give her the benefit of the doubt.

"Right here." She waved at the cat. "Tell the nice detective I was home all night with you. You even woke me up at two a.m. to feed your sorry butt. And you gripe at me for eating too much."

What in the hell was she talking about? It didn't matter. This was not how he expected this to go, and he wasn't sure how to proceed. Odd. Considering he never faltered in his actions. They were always clear and concise. Quick to decide.

"This is a cat, Ms. Duncan."

She nodded vigorously. "She's a sassy one, too. I'm not too surprised she's ignoring you. She doesn't like many people, especially men."

Okay. He needed to reevaluate and question his gut. Maybe she did kill her boss. She was clearly not firing on all cylinders right now.

They were having some kinky sex. Things got out of hand. She hadn't meant to strangle the guy. He could put in a good word for her with the DA's office.

"Not good enough. As sorry as I am she won't answer my question, I can't take the word of a cat that you were home all night."

What the hell?

What did he just say?

He should be laying into her and demanding she tell him where she really was last night. Because this situation was too odd.

Her bottom lip started to wobble. Then she trembled and went rigid as if forcing her emotions back. Thank God. The last thing he needed was a weeping—crazy—woman on his hands.

"Look, I was home alone all night. And yes, with my cat, Willow. I did not kill my boss, even though I hated the man."

Her eyes bulged that she even uttered that. It made him want to chuckle. She had no filter. It was refreshing. Most people put on the best show they could with him. Lied through their teeth like he wouldn't catch on. He always caught on.

"Why did you hate him?"

She pressed her lips together as if that would hold back more words.

"Ms. Duncan?" he said softly, something he never did with people. But for some reason—he didn't want to dig into the reason why—he felt like he needed to tread gently with her.

She shrugged. "He had grabby hands I didn't appreciate." She looked away, reaching down to pet her cat on the back.

Another interesting tidbit. Rory wondered how many other women Mr. Fontain might've had grabby hands with. Perhaps the woman he had been with last night had been a hooker or escort of some kind.

"How grabby?"

Geez. He was even speaking her odd language. What was wrong with him?

Her eyes reconnected with his. "Too...grabby. Do you want a doughnut? I have the best doughnuts."

Then she walked away with quick steps where he had no choice but to follow.

Meow.

Rory jerked at the sudden sound.

Meow.

Shaking his head, he walked around the cat, but stopped and looked back at it. He refused to believe the cat was talking to him.

"I don't speak cat. Keep your distance."

But he also wouldn't be threatened by a cat.

AFTER WIPING her face and neck with a dishtowel—it was all she had on hand at the moment—she snatched another doughnut. She didn't even care she told herself to stay away from the bag the rest of the day. Well, she had jogged to make up for scarfing the other ones.

But she didn't care.

The nasty detective was asking questions, looking at her funny, and making her nerves skyrocket. It was a terrible habit, but she ate when she was stressed. Or threw on the sappiest, saddest movie she could find and balled her eyes out—which she couldn't do at the moment with the terrible detective in her house. Not the best way to relieve her stress, but it made her feel better to think she was crying over the movie and not her sad, pitiful life.

A throat cleared.

She looked up from the bag, her hand hidden inside.

Damn. She hadn't even had a chance to grab a doughnut and stuff it down her throat before he came in.

"Ms. Duncan—"

"Brooke is fine. No need for formalities." It reminded her of her aunt that she never got along with. No, thanks. Didn't need that reminder at a time like this.

Then she drew two doughnuts out and held her hand toward him. "Doughnut?"

He stepped closer, his brows puckered as if he might take a doughnut.

Until Willow screeched, jumped on his leg, dug her claws in, and then raced around the kitchen before stopping by her feet.

"Shit. Damn cat." Detective Walker rubbed his leg, then groaned. "Your cat attacked me." His irritated gaze met hers. "She ripped my pants."

Brooke leaned over the island counter a bit and grimaced at the small tear in his nice gray pants.

Whoopsies. Well, it's not like she had control over Willow. Sure, she bought Willow, gave her a home, but that cat never listened to her. Willow lived in her world and expected everyone to follow her rules.

She didn't know what to say. So, she brought a doughnut to her mouth and demolished it in one bite.

Meow.

Brooke looked down at Willow, arched a brow—silently begging her to knock it off—then shot her gaze back to the detective.

Still chewing a bit of the doughnut, she said, "There's your alibi. Willow's always straightforward in her communication."

A slow, seductive—the man had the most delectable lips to look at—smile appeared. "I can't tell if you're plain crazy or scared about something."

Whoa! Her mind veered completely off course there.

Why was she thinking about his lips in any manner? And her? Crazy? Only on Tuesdays because it was garbage day and she had a weird thing about touching the garbage can.

She shivered thinking about it.

"Do you know something?" He paused, stepping closer to the counter. "You can tell me anything, Brooke."

She knew nothing. Shock still coursed through her veins that her asshole, jerk-off boss was dead. Sure, she hated the guy, but she would never wish anyone dead, no matter how terrible of a person they were.

"Doughnut?" She held out her hand again with the remaining doughnut still sitting there. The powdered sugar was a bit melted and one side was crushed. She might've been squeezing her hand, especially when he moved closer to the counter.

"No, thanks." He smiled. A full-blown smile that had her squishing the doughnut in her hand and grabbing the counter with her free hand to keep herself upright.

Talk about knocking her off her feet. The man's smile lit up the room and enhanced his already handsome features.

"Tell me about your last interaction with your boss."

Despite his smile, her insides gurgled with unease. She did not want to talk about anything. Definitely not about her boss. She had no idea who murdered him, but it wasn't her.

"I should fix your pants. That was so rude of Willow. Take them off. I'll patch it up."

Low laughter echoed between them as his lips split into a charming grin. "I can honestly say I've never met anyone who surprises me every time they speak."

Oh, dear.

Her and stress...yeah, it didn't mix well at all.

She brought her hand filled with the crushed doughnut

to her mouth and chomped down on all the pieces. Even licked her hand to get all the crumbs, making sure each piece disappeared. Very unladylike. She could even hear her aunt's nasally voice in her ear, berating her for such an insolent action.

Just one of the many reasons when she did date, the guy didn't last long. She had too many weird intricacies they couldn't handle. Well, except Ted. He didn't like it when she broke it off last week.

Look up the word awkward, and you'd find a picture of her in all its glory.

"If I take my pants off...for you to fix the rip," he said with a wink, "will you answer my questions?"

Oh, dear, dear, dear.

What had she gotten herself into?

Because she wanted to say, "Yes. Take your pants off."

Then add, "Do me now."

SHIT. He hadn't had this much fun in a long time. Especially interviewing a potential suspect—now witness. There was no way this woman killed her boss.

The cat?

Hell, yes. That demon spawn holy terror definitely could've bludgeoned her boss to death, if the man would've died by blunt force trauma, that is.

Maybe he was as crazy as Brooke for even thinking such a thing.

And for suggesting he take his pants off. He was *not* taking his pants off.

She bit her bottom lip, her eyes round. A mixture of

shock and contemplation, as if considering his outlandish question.

He had been joking.

Sort of.

His gut was telling him it wouldn't be a bad thing to take his pants off. Then take her shorts off.

She intrigued him. Kept him on his toes. And oddly enough, he found that very attractive. It'd been a long time since he'd been with a woman. After his ex—who he wished he wouldn't even think about for a second—he had given up on the dating scene. Too much hassle. He should've never even married her in the first place. Divorce was a messy business.

"Brooke, you don—"

"Okay. I'll answer your questions if you let me fix the rip."

Whoa. He hadn't expected that.

"Seriously?"

"Yep!" Then she smiled brightly. "Be right back. Have a seat in the living room."

He didn't follow her as she walked—more like sprinted —out of the kitchen. But he hesitated before making his way to the living room where he sat down.

What the hell was he doing?

He was by the book. Straight and narrow. Did his job and did it damn well, by following all the rules.

He should be following her, making sure she wasn't going for some sort of weapon and offing him like she could've offed her boss. If she walked into the room with a tie, suggesting naughty sexy things, he knew he had his killer.

But he had already concluded—his gut screamed it— that she hadn't murdered her boss. Which was why his heart didn't stutter with trepidation that she was getting a weapon. No, it was more along the lines of what would happen when she walked into the room.

Was he really going to take his pants off in front of a woman he barely knew?

Shit. If Reese knew he was even following her directions, he would never hear the end of it. It'd be something he'd put in his stupid mental box for safekeeping where he could pull it out at any time for shits and giggles. He hated when Reese said shit like that to him. "Putting this in my mental box. Never going to forget it." He always wanted to punch him in the face when he said it, and in that nauseatingly sly voice with a damn smirk on his lips.

Meow.

Rory flinched as Willow jumped on the coffee table in front of him, and then sat down. And stared. Hard.

"Shoo! I don't like cats, and I certainly don't like you." He even braved waving his hands at her, but she didn't even flinch, not like he had at her sudden intrusion.

Yep. Round one to Willow. Damn, aggravating cat.

Meow.

"Yeah, yeah, I heard your alibi for Brooke the first time. Got it. She didn't do it."

Willow's tail moved gracefully back and forth, then she laid down and stretched her body, her paws dangling in his direction.

"Okay. I should leave my card on this table and go. I'm talking to a dumb cat, who doesn't respect personal space." He leaned closer. "You don't. I asked you to move."

She moved her paws a little as if tempting him to touch and play with her.

He shook his head as he leaned back on the couch.

"Here we go," Brooke said with a chipper voice as she walked into the room.

He sat up straight and knew right away his opportunity was lost. He should've left when he had the chance. Because the tender, yet terrified smile on her face was hard to look away from. The woman mesmerized him with the littlest things and he couldn't figure out why.

"Look, Brooke, I don—"

Then she pushed the coffee table slightly, which made Willow meow and jump up from her spot and saunter away. Thank God for small miracles. But then Brooke continued to surprise him when she set a small box full of sewing supplies on the table and grabbed the side of his pants.

"Don't move. I don't want to nick you."

Then her hand slid up his pants as she grabbed a needle already threaded from the box.

"You don't have to take them off. See. I can fit my hand in there."

She paused and looked up at him.

He couldn't tear his eyes away, or say anything. Her hand was cold against his skin. He could feel a slight tremble. He wasn't sure if it was coming from her...or him.

Hell, he didn't mind if she fit her hand in other parts of his pants.

He watched as her throat moved as she swallowed hard. Yep, he felt the same way. The air felt electrified. Like one small movement and everything would explode—in the most enticing way.

Then the moment shattered when she averted her gaze and started sewing.

"So, ask away? What do you want to know about my grabby hands boss?"

Hmm. One point to Brooke. She said she'd sew his pants

while he asked questions. Yet, he felt like he should uphold his part of the bargain and take his pants off, even though she said he didn't have to. He really, really wanted to.

"Let's start at the beginning. I want to know everything."

He had no pressing urge to leave anymore. She was barely touching him, only her cold hand brushing against his skin now and again, but it was enough to put him in a trance and keep his ass plastered in the seat until the end of time.

3

WRITING PROMPT ~ MMM...
THAT CAT HAS TO GO.

O. M. G. Could he feel her shaky hands? Because her nerves were riled so high, she wanted to puke. And she only ever threw up when she was near sushi. The smell, the sight...ugh, even the thought of sushi made her insides gurgle with unease.

That's how she felt right now with her hand up Detective Walker's pants.

Well, not literally. She'd have to drag her hand farther up to *really* be in his pants. Much, much farther up.

"Brooke?"

"Mmm..." She shook her head, realizing how that came out. Then looked up at him. "Hmm? What is it?"

He eyed her funny, although with a sexy-as-sin grin as if he found her humorous. Unfortunately, she didn't think in a good way. No man ever looked at her with hunger in his eyes. Well, they did when staring at her chest. Dumb big boobs. But a I-want-you-with-every-breath-in-my-body kind of hunger? Yeah, that never happened. She totally had to be misinterpreting his expression.

"I said I wanted to know everything." His brow rose. Not

cockishly. Geez, was that even a word? It sounded like a word. She was going with it was a word, and she'd use it at work one day just to prove it. But his brow arched in a way that said he would wait all day if she so chose to keep him waiting.

"About?"

His brow inched up a little more.

Duh! Right. Her dead, murdered boss and his now not-so-grabby hands.

"Right. My boss. Umm...yeah. He was a jerk of the highest order and..." And she shouldn't have said she'd talk about her boss. Her eyes snapped back to his pants to finish the last few loops she needed to complete to get as far away from the yummy temptation sitting in front of her.

Willow would not be getting her nightly treat for this. How dare she put Brooke in this position. Sewing a man's pants. Feeling his sweet skin. Tempting her to want to sin with him when she swore off men after her last doozy.

She hated her boss. She had nothing nice to say about him. The last thing she needed was this detective even pondering the idea she killed him. She would not do well in jail. Orange looked terrible on her. Made her look like a frumpy pumpkin, no matter the style of shirt or dress she tried on.

"And..."

For heaven's sake. No man should be devilishly handsome and have a voice that melted like butter when he spoke.

She stitched the last stitch, looped and tied a knot, and grabbed the scissors from her sewing box, snipping the thread as if she had been born to sew. She hesitated to remove her hand from his pants but knew nothing good would come from this man being so close to her. And remaining in her house. He had to leave. Now.

"And I'm all done."

Her hand slid out of his pants, shaking. Steeling her nerves, she tossed the scissors and needle in the box and was about to stand up and move as far away from him as she could when a hand to her cheek stopped her cold.

"Look at me."

In his silky smooth voice, it sounded like a soft caress to kindly do as he bid. But she knew it had been far from a request. It had been a demand. It was impossible to ignore.

She slowly tilted her gaze his way. Nothing but patience echoed back. Although she had felt a standoffish behavior when he first introduced himself, she felt nothing of the sort now. How odd he could flip such a switch.

It should be a clue for her to stay as far away from him as possible.

"It's okay. I promise." His hand drifted away from her cheek—she missed his touch immediately—and he patted the spot next to him. "Sit by me."

This time she heard more of a request rather than a demand, which had her obeying a little faster. She didn't like demands. Being treated like a servant. She had feelings. She could do as she pleased. Something Ted didn't agree with either. *Hello, jerkwad, not my husband. Barely even my long-time boyfriend.* Three months didn't classify him to be her boss and keeper.

Her butt plopped down next to him with her eyes still glued to his. She was afraid to look away and she wasn't even sure why. Something crackled between them. An odd sort of tension she wasn't used to feeling.

"Let's not start at the beginning. Let's start with yesterday. What happened?"

She swallowed, hating to relive any part of it. Hadn't she already told him what happened? Sort of. He had grabby hands. What more did he want?

"My boss is between girlfriends. He thinks when he's available, it's okay to hit on any woman within a one-foot radius. Unfortunately, I'm in that radius a lot, as his secretary. He's normally crude with his words, but this time he put...he touched my butt. Slapped it." She licked her lips, hoping to occupy her mouth with something other than more talking. That should be enough to satisfy him.

His eyes zeroed in on the action, an intensity sizzling in their depths.

She stopped licking her lips.

He inhaled heavily and didn't respond right away.

"What happened after that?" His jaw clenched as he asked.

"Well." She rolled her eyes upward, staring at the ceiling for a moment. "I sort of reacted by...you know...slapping him back." Her eyes bulged. "On the cheek. In anger. Of course. Not on his ass."

The fierce look on his face disappeared as a sensual smile popped up. "Good for you. Did you report it?"

She swallowed again, hating her weakness. "No. Look, I didn't kill him. He was one of the worst human beings I've ever met, but I didn't kill him. I can't even touch raw meat. Like, cut it or anything. Gross. There's no way I could kill someone."

He chuckled. "So, do you even eat meat?"

"Yeah." She didn't elaborate as she didn't want to confess her methods because he would think her even more insane than he already did.

"There's something about you, Brooke. I don't know

what it is. You make me..." He started to lean closer as if he wanted to kiss her.

Oh, yes, please. She wouldn't say no to a kiss, even though it would be a terrible idea.

"I make you, what?"

His lips inched closer. "You make me—"

"Shit!"

Brooke winced. Willow had jumped on his lap, digging her claws in. Right on the spot every man coveted.

HE IMAGINED the face he was making right now wasn't pretty. But neither was the pain. That damn cat...

What did it have against him? He thought he was nice enough a few minutes ago. Telling her he knew Brooke didn't have anything to do with the murder.

Rory blew out a deep breath, his eyes closed as he held his hands over his crotch. Yeah, not a pretty sight at all, but hell, he needed to protect his crown jewels. He couldn't risk another sneak attack. He got the message loud and clear.

No kissing.

But damn... He still wanted to. When he definitely shouldn't.

"Detective..." Brooke whispered. "Are you okay?"

Nope. He was not okay. He couldn't even find his voice. One, because he wanted to shout nasty, vulgar words at a cat. Two, because the pain hadn't subsided yet.

Sure, getting hit in the balls was painful. Like getting the wind knocked right out of you.

But claws attaching to—and sinking in—that was another pain entirely. It honestly had no words.

"Should I get some ice?" Brooke's voice was still low and

soft as if talking to a toddler verging on the start of a massive tantrum. "What do you need?"

Well, for all the pain he was enduring, he needed that kiss. A kiss he shouldn't even want.

"That cat has to go," he croaked. Then he cracked open his eyes, finding Brooke's concerned gaze. "Or I can go. But we can't talk with the cat in the vicinity anymore."

Brooke nodded, biting her bottom lip.

Yeah, nope. She shouldn't bite her lip. It enticed him to get closer. To take a little nibble himself.

She didn't indicate what her nod meant. Yes, the cat would be banished? God, yes, he hoped so. Or, yes, he should go? Not the answer he wanted, but it would be the wiser one.

Rory shifted on the couch, wincing, yet the pain was starting to ebb away. Slightly.

"Willow..." Brooke smiled as if that would lessen whatever horrible thing she was about to say. Rory had no doubt he wouldn't like what she was about to say. "She doesn't listen very well. She has a mind of her own."

"She's a cat."

Pick her up and put her in another room and close the door. Seemed simple enough to him.

Brooke frowned.

Rory didn't like the way her brows dipped and her smile disappeared. He couldn't figure out why she frowned either —or why it bothered him so much.

"She's not just a cat."

He chuckled, regretting the decision immediately when Brooke's frown worsened.

"She's family. And I could ask her nicely to go to another room, but I won't put her in another room."

It didn't take detective skills to read between the lines.

"So, in other words, you can't pick her up because she'll attack you like she attacked my balls."

"Well, I can pick her up," Brooke averted her gaze, "but it's not always a pretty sight."

"I imagine my balls aren't either at the moment."

That garnered a delightful laugh out of Brooke. Shit. He'd keep making fun of himself if he got to hear more of that sweet sound.

What was this woman doing to him?

Putting him under a spell, for sure. He never acted this way with a woman. After his ex-wife took his heart and used it like it was a bullseye for target practice, he wasn't ready to give another woman a chance to do the same thing.

She made him lose his mind. Which was what he had been trying to say before the demon spawn cat nearly eviscerated his balls. It was a good thing he never spoke those words. Getting any closer to this woman—beautiful, tempting woman—would not be good.

"I should go."

With that decision firmly planted, he stood up. A sharp pain rattled up his spine, then withered away until only a dull ache remained.

That damn, damn cat.

"Of course." Brooke stood up as well. "Was there anything else I can help you with?"

Case-wise, he didn't think so. With the information she had given him—brief as it may be—he had a good start to work with. He imagined her boss had many enemies that would want him dead, especially if he had such grabby hands.

Personal-wise, she could help him in so many ways.

But he wasn't looking for a woman in his life. And not one with a murderous cat that was considered family.

"I'll drop by if there's anything else I need. If you think of anything else, give me a call." He grabbed a card from his wallet and set it on the coffee table.

No need to invite trouble by making even the slightest contact. One touch and he'd lose his mind and kiss her, risking the wrath of Willow.

No, thanks.

"Thank you for your time, Brooke."

Then he walked out of the room, hating himself for how abrupt that sounded.

What a jackass.

Willow stood by the door as he approached it.

"I'm leaving. You got your way, demon spawn."

Meow.

Rory didn't stick around to hear more. He whipped open the door and left, feeling like a fool.

Letting a dumb cat run him out of the house. How ridiculous. He'd never live it down if his partner found out.

4

WRITING PROMPT ~ ON SECOND
THOUGHT. NOT AGAIN…

BROOKE CURLED UNDER THE BLANKET, petting Willow immediately as she jumped up on the couch and took a spot right on her lap above the blanket. She had decided to sit on the couch for a small moment to collect her thoughts. Now she'd be here a while because she hated shoving off Willow. She'd rather sit here for an hour than push Willow off her lap. Plus, when she petted Willow, she purred, and the melodic sound always put Brooke at ease, especially when she was stressed.

After the day she had, stress didn't even begin to describe how she felt.

Since the moment the detective left hours ago, her mind had been circling with thought after thought.

Disgusting memories of her boss. How she wasn't sad he was dead. Which made her feel like a terrible person, even though her boss had been a true nightmare and not worthy of her guilt.

Of course, enticing thoughts of Detective Walker and how depressing it was he didn't get the chance to kiss her.

Her hand paused petting Willow. All her fault she didn't get to taste his decadent lips. Stopping didn't sway Willow. She nudged her hand, indicating she wanted more rubs along the stretch of her back. She loved little rubs under her neck, on top of her head, and down her back, but she wasn't a fan of her belly. Brooke made sure to stay clear of that area.

She rubbed vigorously under her chin, laughing. "You silly kitty. You should apologize for ruining the moment. I bet he is a fantastic kisser."

Willow didn't respond other than to nudge her hand again to keep going, her purr loud and soothing.

"Yeah, on second thought..." Brooke shook her head. "No good would come from kissing that man. I'm not even sure I liked him. He could be a bit abrasive and in-your-face, you know. I've had enough of those kinds of guys."

Another gentle prod to her hand was the only answer she got, which she took to mean Willow agreed with her.

She continued to sit on her couch, petting Willow, her mind going in a million different directions. She'd have to get up and make supper soon. She simply didn't have the energy. After everything that happened today, she didn't have the energy for much. Not even going to work tomorrow.

How terrible would it be if she called in sick again? Would they think she had something to do with her boss's murder?

She sat up straight, which jolted Willow out of her lap.

Did they already think she had something to do with it? She called out today, not knowing her boss had been found murdered. They could think she did it on purpose to avoid the situation.

Leaning slowly against the couch, she tried to dispel the

silly notion. But couldn't. She knew the detective had even thought of her as a potential suspect. Why wouldn't her co-workers think the same thing? She had left last night upset. Although she had tried to hold her emotions in, she was positive people got the drift she didn't leave happy.

Then she called out of work.

Oh, dear.

Not good at all.

She stood up, grabbing her phone from the coffee table, and continued to stand there, unsure of how to proceed. Who did she call? And what would she say?

I didn't kill him. I swear.

That sounded dumb. And slightly guilty, like she was trying too hard to hide the truth.

This was ridiculous. She was acting ridiculous. No one thought she killed her boss. He was a jackass to everyone. There were so many possible suspects.

With that thought—not exactly firmly planted in her mind—she decided now was a good time to make supper. She slid the phone into her pocket. Although, she didn't think she'd have an appetite for much, so a light salad sounded nice.

Brooke took her time grabbing the ingredients: romaine lettuce, cut-up carrots, a boiled egg sliced, a toss of sunflower seeds, topped with Caesar dressing. Yum! Her mouth salivated as her bowl overflowed with everything.

Her fork nearly made it to her mouth for the first wonderful bite when her doorbell went off.

"I hope it's not that detective again."

Yet, as she walked toward the front door, she knew she uttered a lie. A part of her hoped it was him. She wanted that kiss still, no matter how much she shouldn't.

When she looked through the peephole, she didn't see

anyone. Opening the door, her brows pleated as she looked around the porch and her front yard. No vehicle sat parked in her driveway. No person or animal—not that she thought an animal would push the doorbell—was anywhere in sight. But it was good to check for every possible thing.

Odd.

Closing the door, she turned around and jumped.

Willow sat in the middle of the hallway, staring up at her.

Meow.

Brooke looked down the hallway that led to the kitchen, the hairs suddenly standing up on her arms.

Then she looked at Willow, who had stood up.

Meow.

"You're right. It's weird the doorbell went off and no one's out there. What should we do?"

Willow walked up and rubbed against her leg. The same leg that held her phone in her pocket.

It wasn't the smartest idea that popped in her head, but she had the strangest feeling something was about to happen, and not in a good way. Heading upstairs, the fastest she had ever done, she went straight for her room, shutting the door as soon as Willow came inside as well. Which further confirmed her suspicions something was wrong. Well, okay, maybe she was overreacting a little bit because Willow followed her around the house most of the time. Such a pushy cat, never respecting boundaries.

But she always liked to be safer than sorry. Something her dad had loved to say to her as a child growing up.

Pulling out her phone, she found Detective Walker's number. Because, yeah, she totally saved his number the minute he left. So pathetic.

Then she hit dial.

RORY FIDDLED with the beer label on the bottle, trying to ignore Reese's snickering. He should've never told him about Brooke and everything that occurred. Yeah, sure, he had to tell Reese about what she said about her boss, but everything else? Should've kept it zipped up. Reese was having way too much fun at his expense.

"How are your balls now? Should I get Tank to get you an ice pack?" Reese asked softly as if talking to a child—but of course, the snickering behind each word told him he wasn't being serious.

Funny enough, Rory wouldn't say no to an ice pack. His balls still had a lingering pain. Hello! Claws dug into his skin. That shit hurt.

"Are you done yet?"

Reese shrugged. "Maybe. Maybe not. But I'm putting this in my mental box. Never going to forget it."

"You are the worst best friend in the entire world."

"Yet, you'd be lost without me." Reese winked, then clinked bottles with his. "You going to drink that, or just keep playing with the damn label?"

He didn't look at Reese. Any sort of eye contact would be his downfall. His partner—and yeah, his best friend of fifteen years—would see the truth.

He liked Brooke. Crazy cat lady, and although not a suspect, definitely a witness in a murder investigation.

"You could always feign some more questions and drop by her place. Get that kiss you didn't manage to get the first time around. Lock the cat in a dungeon or something. Far, far away from your balls."

Rory couldn't hold back chuckling along with Reese,

even though it wouldn't be funny if Willow sunk her claws into him again. No, thanks.

Just one more reason why Reese would always be his best friend, no matter how much he wanted to hate him sometimes. Because he knew the heart of the problem without even needing to make eye contact. Damn him.

"It wouldn't work. No, thanks."

"Shit. Not again," Reese muttered.

"What?" Rory looked around the small dingy bar they liked to venture to after a long day's work. It was around the block from the precinct, sort of hidden from the main drag. One had to enter through the alleyway, so unless a person knew about the location, people passed by it. It didn't make Rory sad because he liked it better when it wasn't busy. Sometimes, trouble did walk in, and Tank, who ran the bar, always appreciated it more when he and Reese stepped in to take care of the problem. Not that Tank couldn't handle any problems his way—former military, he could handle anything. But he also liked to fly under the radar, so letting them step in was always on top of Tank's list.

Reese whacked him on the back of the head. "You're being an idiot."

He rubbed the back of his head, finally glancing at Reese with a menacing glare. "What the hell was that for?"

"To knock some sense into you. You always do this with women. You find a potentially good one—one you really like—but instead of doing something about it, like asking her out like a man, you walk away, creating issues in your head that it would never work out."

"I do not. And did you forget about Dawn? You know, my crazy ex-wife. I gave her a chance, and look what she did."

"You've been divorced over six months. It's time to move

on. The few potential women you've met, they could've been keepers, and you didn't give them a chance."

"After Dawn, I like to be cautious. Sure, it's been six months, but it's not like she's completely out of my life."

Reese had his hand ready like he wanted to slap him again. "You didn't sleep with your ex-wife, did you? Who knows what diseases she could have."

Rory shivered from the thought. Hell, no, he hadn't slept with her. Shit. Before the divorce, and even before he found out she had been shacking up with the neighbor, it had been a while for them. Maybe that's why she ventured to new pastures. He'd be the first to admit, he worked too much. But she could've communicated with him about his lack of affections instead of sleeping with the next-door neighbor.

"Eww, no. I haven't. She's been calling lately."

"Why?"

Rory shrugged, hoping to dispel the conversation. He'd rather talk about Brooke and her lunatic cat.

"She after more money?"

Ha! That bitch wasn't getting any more money out of him. Thankfully, she hadn't gotten a ton out of the divorce, which had pissed her off. Hello, cheated. He got the best divorce lawyer out there to make sure he came out looking good in the divorce. He got the house, which he sold right away. Not a chance he wanted to continue to live next to the asshole who screwed his wife. He had been tempted to put a bullet in him just on the principle of the matter. They had separate banking accounts, thank goodness. No money was split in regards to that. She attempted to get alimony payments from him, but he got a good judge. Didn't need to go down that route. Yet, Dawn was exactly like she always was, even when he met her, which should've been a clue. A money-hungry whore.

He had tried to be a good husband. Buying her nice things, expensive jewelry. Yet, being a detective didn't yield tons of money. Not even a year into the marriage things started to turn sour when he put a stop to it. The gap between them widened until she finally went looking for new blood. Their neighbor had been a doctor.

Well, sorry, but this ship had sailed, and he wasn't about to cave in to her charms. Oh, and he knew she thought she was being sexy and alluring every time she called—but she wasn't. It always made him sick to his stomach and have a hard time sleeping.

"Probably. She won't stop calling, and I'm starting to get annoyed."

"Restraining order?"

Rory chuckled. "Oh, she'd get a kick out of that."

"Screw that bitch."

Rory's thoughts exactly.

"So, this Brooke chick? Man up."

"Umm...murdered boss. Investigation. Witness. Need I say more?"

Although, Rory wouldn't dispute anything Reese said earlier about him avoiding women, especially a potentially good one. It was all true. But hell, he was sick of women putting him through the wringer. It was easier to avoid them. He had even waited until he was thirty-seven to get married, not wanting to pick the wrong one. Yet, he had. Perhaps he had rushed into marriage with Dawn because he had felt his life flashing before his eyes. Quite a few friends finding the love of their lives, getting married, having kids, and what was he doing? Dating here and there and getting older each day. Two years later, now divorced, nearing the big four-oh, he felt that noose around his neck that time was slipping away once again.

Brooke owned the demon cat from hell. That should be enough of a reason to stay as far away as possible, no matter how much older he was getting.

"Excuses. But whatever, it's your balls not getting tender loving care, not mine." Then Reese took a sip of beer, looking away as if the conversation was over.

Rory laughed. Because Reese wasn't getting any loving care to his balls either. Neither of them had dated in a while. Maybe Rory should twist the conversation around and focus on Reese's dating life instead. See how he liked it.

Before he could snap back, his phone rang. Pulling it out of his pocket, he didn't recognize the number, but that didn't mean anything. He got calls all the time from people he didn't know, usually pertaining to a case.

"This is Detective Walker."

"I need you. I think. I don't know actually. The doorbell went off and I checked it, but no one was there. Then Willow had the same weird feeling as me, so we went upstairs, and now I'm afraid to go back down there."

Well, it didn't take a genius to figure out who was on the other line, even though she didn't say hello or identify herself.

Brooke had a way about her that made it easy to decipher who it was. Plus, he'd never forget her voice. Soft and smooth with, unfortunately, a hint of fear.

"Is someone in the house? Did you hear anything?"

"No and no. At least, I think the first question is a no. Someone rang the doorbell, but nobody was there. That's odd, isn't it?"

"Yeah—"

"Okay, so you'll come over and do a sweep of the house? Is that how you say it? Or check the perimeter? I don't know the lingo."

Rory had to suppress a laugh. This woman never failed to surprise him. And she loved to talk—or one could call it babbling. But she had interrupted before he could say, "Yeah, but it could be a bunch of teenagers having fun or something."

He decided not to say it at all. She sounded scared.

And Reese was right—the bastard. He did want that kiss. Brooke didn't seem anything like his ex. She seemed down-to-earth and like she cared more about things than just herself. Definitely not self-absorbed like Dawn.

"Where are you upstairs? In your bedroom?"

"Yes, with the door locked."

Perfect place to kiss.

"I'll be right there." He couldn't stop the smile from spreading across his lips. "To check the perimeter and make a sweep of the house."

He hung up after reassuring Brooke a few more times he'd be right there.

"I actually thought there might be a problem with your lady love, but with the shit-eating grin on your face, Brooke needs to think about what you said and read between the lines."

Rory stood up, shoving his phone in his pocket. "Shut up."

"Have fun sweeping the house and checking that perimeter," Reese said with a double wink.

"I will, asshole." Then Rory whacked him on the back of the head and left.

He drove fast. For two reasons. One, in case there was an actual problem. Two, because he was dying for that kiss.

When he got to her house, everything looked fine in the driveway and her yard. Although, as he neared her front door, his gut started to churn.

The door was slightly ajar.

Brooke didn't mention that.

5

WRITING PROMPT ~ BLUE BALLS. BIRDS.

"Did you hear that? Because I heard it." Brooke snuggled Willow closer to her chest. Although, Willow wasn't appreciating the hug, as she wiggled and squirmed in her arms. Enough so that Brooke had no choice but to let go.

"Well, you are no help in comfort right now. Talk about selfish. I always pet you when you decide to walk on my chest at night, looking for rubs when I'm sleeping," Brooke said, trying to prove her point how one-sided this relationship was. "So rude. There is possibly a serial killer in this house, and you won't even sit by me."

Willow meowed, then jumped back on the bed, coming closer until she touched her hand, looking for a rub. Typical of her. She wouldn't let her hug her, but oh no, Brooke had to pet her on demand.

Yet, Brooke couldn't deny her, especially since she was scared at the moment. The whole doorbell incident was freaking her out, and even more so when Detective Walker didn't tell her it wasn't a big deal. Which totally meant it was. With the way her mind weaved stories in a heartbeat, it wasn't looking good for her stress-o-meter. It was skyrocketing to the eat-a-full-container-of-ice-cream instead of eat-a-bowl-of-ice-cream. With extra fudge and chopped nuts for a topping.

"What is taking him so long?"

Willow didn't answer except to nudge her hand to keep petting.

"Yeah, yeah, you're just as excited to see him as me." She paused, reciting the words in her mind.

Excited to see him?

Then she giggled. Yeah, she was excited to see him. She wanted that kiss Willow thwarted. Ugh. Another example of her selfishness.

She leaned down, eliciting an annoyed meow from Willow as she hugged her. "I still love you, even though you act like the world revolves around you. Which, I will admit, does here. I can't help myself. I love you and—"

A soft knock on her door startled her so much she shrieked, jumped back, which, because she could be a klutz at times, brought her too close to the corner of the bed. Instead of jumping and falling on the mattress, she tumbled off the side, dropping hard to the floor. A loud moan escaped as Willow hissed and scrambled into the master bathroom that connected with her bedroom.

"Brooke!"

Before she could respond, her door busted open, cracking and breaking part of the doorframe. Detective Walker stepped through with his gun waving around like a lunatic, his eyes glazed with fear.

"Where are they? Did they hurt you?"

She sat up slowly. "Who?"

He rushed to her side, cupping her chin. "Whoever made you scream. Where are they?"

She glanced around, then started giggling hysterically.

"You made me scream. The knock on the door startled me."
Then she peered around his shoulder and made a pouty
face. "You broke my doorframe."

Detective Walker frowned, glancing behind him, then
back at her. Without a word, he stood up, searched her room
everywhere. Everywhere! From the closet to under the bed
to the bathroom, where he obviously ran into Willow.
Because Brooke heard another hiss, a vicious curse, and
what sounded like her bottles in the shower falling from the
shelf to the tub.

She stood up as he walked back into the bedroom. Her
ass hurt, stinging a little still. She was tempted to rub it
when she met his irate gaze.

Why was he mad at her? She wasn't the one who busted
into her bedroom breaking her door.

He came closer, the fire flashing in his eyes becoming
more intense the closer he got. She had nowhere to go when
he finally stopped in front of her, blocking her between him
and her bed. Which, if not for the anger blazing in his eyes,
wouldn't be such a bad way to box her in.

"I said your name several times, you didn't answer. I then
knocked and said your name again. You screamed."

"And then you broke my door," she replied as she
pointed behind him, brushing her arm against his.

His eyes flashed again. "I did what I had to do. I thought
you were being attacked."

"I wasn't." Then she dropped her hand, brushing his
arm again.

He clenched his jaw. "You should stop touching me."

Oh, snap. He looked beyond pissed. Like he wanted to
rip her to shreds. Well, excuse her. She should be the one
pissed. He broke her door.

"If anyone should be upset here, it should be me. You

broke my door. And I didn't mean to touch your arm. It happened when I was pointing. A total accident. See."

Then she proceeded to demonstrate by raising her hand, pointing, brushing his arm, which couldn't be helped with how close he was standing. Then she dropped her hand, brushing his arm again.

"Don't stand so close if you don't want me to touch you."

He let out a strained breath.

"Well, it's true."

Instead of taking a step back, he took a step forward, forcing her to lean back toward the bed so she didn't touch him. Something he clearly didn't want her to do.

"You think I'm upset?"

"Uh, duh. You sound upset. You look upset. Your face is all rigid and you're all tense. All clear signs of being upset."

He nodded as if all that made sense, yet none of his anger disappeared.

"I just had the worst scare of my life, and trust me, Brooke, I've been in some pretty dangerous situations. I thought you were in danger. This," he said, circling his face, "is not the face of anger. This is the face of terror. For you." Then he dropped his hand, putting it behind her neck, and pulled her closer. "And it's also the look of having blue balls since I left. You do something to me that...shit. I don't like it."

"Umm..." So many things were going through her mind and she didn't know where to start.

"Don't say anything because you likely won't shut up." Then he pulled her the rest of the way toward him, claiming her lips in a searing kiss that set her body on fire.

He said he had blue balls all day?

Oh, she would be happy to take care of that problem. This man and his lips were officially hers. Like when Willow plopped wherever she pleased, claiming the spot without a thought or care, she was claiming his lips. All hers.

She couldn't stop the whiny moan that escaped when he pulled away. But he didn't go far. Resting his forehead against hers with his hand still cupping the back of her neck, he sighed. Heavily.

"What?" she whispered, afraid to even speak.

"I want to keep kissing you, but we do have a problem."

"Oh, God. You're right. I don't have any condoms."

He stood up straight, a wicked grin replacing the forlorn expression he had been wearing. "Not what I had planned to say, but hold the thought for later because I can find some condoms quickly."

She giggled. "Then what?"

He sighed—again. She didn't like it when he sighed.

"Your front door was open when I got here. Did you forget to close it?"

Holy. Shit.

Wait? Did she? She honestly couldn't remember. But she always thought it was best to err on the side of caution.

"Of course I did. What does that mean?"

His brows puckered low. "That someone was in your house." Then his brows rose. "Which is why I broke down your door when you screamed."

That all made perfect sense.

But what did it mean? Why would someone break into her house? Why would someone murder her boss?

Were the two things related?

———

RORY COULD STILL FEEL his heart pounding against his chest. Could Brooke feel it, too? Did she understand how terrified he had been when he heard her scream? He hadn't lied. He had never felt such fear in his life. Not even the time when he and Reese were involved in an armed robbery, a gun centered on his best friend while he tried to talk the drunken, newly widowed man down from robbing a liquor store. Yeah, not the guy's best day. Nor for him and Reese. It had been terrifying, sending all his wits and bravery to the forefront.

But this.

That moment he heard her scream.

A thousand times worse.

With Reese, he knew his enemy. He saw the problem standing in front of him. A guy with a gun, unhinged. Broken beyond despair from losing the love of his life.

This, with Brooke, was a mystery. Okay, he was a detective; mysteries were sort of his thing. But he didn't particularly like mysteries. At least, not when it involved someone he cared about. He didn't care what anyone would say or think. He cared about Brooke, even knowing her less than a day.

Shit.

How in the hell did that happen? How did this spunky, sassy, outrageously gorgeous, funny woman get under his skin so easily?

Well, whatever. Not something he had the time to ponder at the moment. No. He had to figure out who scared the shit out of Brooke by knocking on her door, then entered her house to do...well, that was the million-dollar question, wasn't it? To do what? Hurt her? Scare her? Steal from her?

He pressed her closer, kissing her softly. One, because he wanted to stop the slight trembles he felt coating her body after telling her someone had been in her house. Two, because he needed to stop the terror from running rampant through his veins. He still couldn't get his heartbeat to settle down.

This was insane, the way he felt. But he was going to do what he did in any given situation: roll with it. When it came to intense situations, odd ones, or even crazy ones, the best course of action was always to go with the flow and figure the problem out afterward. Overthinking, overanalyzing, and scrutinizing a situation did nothing but give him a headache. That's what Reese was for. Reese did the over-thinking and overanalyzing. He did the impulsive things.

Maybe he should call him.

Then he immediately discredited the idea. He had to get his entire wits—his racing heart—back to normal before he called his partner. The last thing he wanted was Reese to give him shit in front of Brooke. It was bad enough he had done it without her around.

Hating it, but knowing he had to, he broke the kiss, then smiled when she produced an adorable pouty face. Shit. He would've never in a million years thought a woman making a pouty face would be adorable. But on Brooke, oh so damn adorable. It made him want to lean in for another kiss. And another. And another until he forgot about those condoms they needed and showed her how serious he was about her.

Because that was another thing about him. When he made a decision, he made it quick and decisive, and he didn't budge from it. Look at how he married a self-absorbed woman and got divorced just as fast.

Well, he made another swift decision. He decided Brooke was his.

"We need to talk about this."

She nodded, her eyes widening some. "I'm clean. I haven't even had sex in a while. A long while. Okay, fine, I confess, it's been over a year." Then she looked away, a blush rising on her cheeks. "I can't believe I said that. I mean, sure, I dated Ted for three months, but we never had sex. I wasn't feeling it with him. He was cute and everything, but there were some things—"

Rory couldn't help but chuckle as he put a finger over her mouth to stop her. She blurted out the most random things at the oddest times. He enjoyed it. Most of the time it was truth and honesty spilling out, and he coveted those two traits like a kid on Halloween protecting their bucket of candy.

He gently tugged on her chin to look at him. "Not the conversation I meant, but I'm clean, too. It's been..." He paused, trying to think. After Dawn—bitch from hell—he had sworn off women, which had included sex. "Shit, maybe close to a year like you. A bit less."

Brooke tilted her head as a sweet smile graced her face. "Are you saying that to be nice?"

"One thing you'll always get with me is honesty." He kissed her soft and tenderly as if sealing his honesty with a signature kiss. "I expect the same thing from you."

Which he had no doubt he'd get with her.

Before this conversation could completely derail, he tightened his hands around her waist and tried to keep his smile, but failed.

"I meant, we need to talk about who might've been in your house." His frown increased when he replayed her entire rambling spiel in his head. "Who's Ted?"

He felt the slight shiver coat her body.

"My ex."

"Since when?" Rory didn't like where this was going. "My first thought was it has to do with your boss. But let's talk about Ted."

"He's...harmless."

"You hesitated." Why did she hesitate?

"He could be a bit...demanding. In-your-face." Brooke tilted her head. "Like you sometimes."

"I am not demanding. Tell me more about this Ted."

Brooke giggled. "Okay, not demanding at all."

Yeah, okay. That did sound a bit forceful, but he didn't like to think of another guy with his Brooke. He cocked a brow when she didn't say anything. He might be coming off as demanding, but he wasn't about to leave without some answers.

She rolled her eyes. "Fine, okay. I met him at the gym. He's a personal trainer. Pump It Up Fitness. He was fun to be with, but also at times, a bit controlling. And Willow didn't like him. I ended it about a week ago. He hasn't gotten the message I guess because he keeps calling."

Rory didn't like the sound of that. Although, sounded a bit like Dawn. Not getting the message. Six months after the divorce, one would think she would. Probably couldn't find a new sugar daddy and thought enough time had passed and he'd be willing once again. Not.

"I'll need Ted's information."

"Why?"

Was she being serious?

"So I can check him out. If he's bothering you, I'll make it stop."

A tender smile filtered onto her face. "Okay."

"Now, let's discuss if this might've been related to your boss, to check off all bases. Any mutual enemies?"

Her eyes bulged. "God, no."

"None? Not even rival competitors?"

"I work at an advertising company. Our rivals don't get that vicious."

Rory's lips split into a grin, especially when she rolled

her eyes as if he had said the world's dumbest thing. "Anyone can get vicious."

Another tremble shifted his way. Shit. He hadn't meant to frighten her with his words, even if they were true.

"Your company has a lot of clients. Perhaps another agency wanted one of your clients. Even the slightest thing could set someone off."

Brooke shrugged again. "I can't think of anyone. We've been working with a few new clients, but there haven't been any concerns that I'm aware of."

"Like who?"

She tilted her head, a gesture he found she liked to do when she pondered something.

"A company that sells birdseed. My boss hated working with them. His latest slogan he sent them was 'Feed the birds, feed the beauty.' Which I tried to tell him didn't have much oomph or make much sense, but he never listened to me. Then there's the company that sells hats. They're kind of weird-looking hats. Covers your ears, but they're not made for warmth. More like a style statement." Brooke grimaced as if she'd never be caught dead wearing one. "It's hard to explain without seeing one. Anyway, his bright idea for that was 'Be bold. Be awesome. Be like the Vikings.' They definitely don't look like a Viking's hat. Then there's—"

He hated to cut her off, but he was getting the picture well. Instead of getting angry or annoyed, something his ex would've done, she pressed her lips harder against his finger he had placed over her mouth to shut her up.

"You said there weren't any concerns. It sounds like your boss wasn't doing his job. That would make for a lot of disgruntled clients."

"Oh, he's like that with everyone. I guess I'm used to it. He's terrible at his job."

"So, how did he still have it?" He would've fired the asshole a long time ago, simply for the way he had treated Brooke. He almost wished the guy wasn't dead so he could kill him himself. That bastard should've never put his hands on her in any way. Well, he'd be able to take his aggression out on Ted.

"Who's the detective here? Me or you?" She giggled. "His father's best friend owns the company. He's like his godfather or something. He gets away with everything—or did. What's crazy, Matthew—the owner—has no idea he slept with his wife. The man was truly disgusting."

Brooke had it right. Who was the detective here? Because after working all day on the case with Reese, they never found that juicy tidbit out. Sleeping with the boss's wife was a very nice motive to kill him. And Brooke knew. Which begged the question, who else knew?

So he asked.

His heart, which had calmed slightly, started to beat like a racehorse once more when Brooke's eyes bulged like round saucers. Why did she look at him like not many people knew? Like this could be the reason someone tried to break into her house. To tie up all loose ends.

Well, not on his watch. And not with his woman.

6

"So, did you spend the night? You never called me last night?"

Rory rolled his eyes as he and Reese made their way to chat with Susan. "Like I'd call you with the details. And no, I didn't spend the night."

He had wanted to. After talking a bit more, they decided to order pizza. Brooke ate her salad she had made and then had two slices of pizza. He liked a woman who wasn't afraid to eat. Dawn had been such a stickler about what she put in her body. It had been annoying as hell, but he had endured it because he thought he had loved her. He saw after one day with Brooke, he never even knew what love meant.

They watched a movie until he couldn't take the death glares from Willow and told Brooke he should head out. He had promised to call her today and see her again, and he told her a good friend of his would stop by soon to fix her doorframe. He hadn't meant to break it.

If she would've had condoms, or if he carried some around in his wallet, he would've begged his way into her bed last night. Except he didn't. He sure did today. Put two in a side pocket and threw the entire condom box in his glove box for backup. He wasn't letting Brooke get away next time.

"Did you at least get that kiss?"

Rory grinned like the devil. "Wouldn't you like to know?" Then he knocked on Susan's door and opened it when he saw her gesture from inside through the window.

"Hey, guys. I'm so glad you popped in this morning. I was going to call you."

The excitement on Susan's face ratcheted up Rory's even more. He'd be seeing Brooke tonight *and* they might have a break in the case. What a great day this was turning out to be.

"Something good?" Reese asked, rubbing his hands in glee.

"How does a strand of hair I found on the bed sound? I also found trace DNA on the tie. I ran the strand of hair for DNA and got a match. Nothing on the tie so far."

Whoa. That rarely happened so perfectly.

"And who's the winner?" Rory asked.

"Starla Cooper."

Reese took the papers Susan held out. "Sounds like a porn name."

"She's actually a teacher at one of the high schools in town. No record. Not even speeding tickets. Perfect citizen."

"So why was her hair found in a creep's bed?" Rory asked, not liking how the puzzle pieces were so crooked and not matching.

"I'm not sure. You'd have to ask her, but one interesting thing about her is her sister was reported missing two years ago."

"Steph Cooper. Seventeen years old. Had a fight with her parents, left home, and was never seen again," Reese said as if reading straight from the papers in his hand.

"I thought this was going to be open and close, and now you're adding more mystery to it, Susan." He might've grumbled it more than he intended.

"Hey, I give you the pieces, you put the rest of the puzzle together." Susan shrugged, maintaining her friendly smile.

"How about the DNA on the tie?" Rory asked. It'd be nice if that matched Starla as well. Open and closed case. His favorite.

"Sorry, no match in the system for that. Suggests there might've been more than one person there. Kinky sex. Might not be that far off the mark."

They thanked her and headed straight for the school. The principal didn't appreciate they asked for Ms. Cooper, one of the most liked teachers in the school. Nice, sweet, and always willing to help people out in a pinch.

They met with her in one of the conference rooms. She looked nervous, fidgety hands, slight pallor to her skin when she walked into the room. Oh, the perfect teacher had something to hide.

Like she murdered a man while having sex.

Eww. Rory actually couldn't picture her with Mr. Fontain. Ms. Cooper had shoulder-length hair, a cute face, with semi-kissable lips. If he hadn't fallen in love with Brooke as fast as he had, he might've been attracted to her.

"How can I help you?" Ms. Cooper asked, her voice a little shaky as she took a seat across from him. Reese sat in the chair closest to her.

"Well, you can start with why a strand of your hair was found in the bed of a man murdered two nights ago?" Rory popped out without preamble.

Her eyes widened in surprise. Reese coughed, a subtle message for Rory to cool it. Yeah, okay, his words weren't smooth and polite, but they could be talking to a murderer right now. Why should he be polite?

"I don't know what you're talking about."

Wow. Interesting. Going with the feigning ignorance defense.

"Ms. Cooper, evidence doesn't lie. If you were with him prior to getting killed, there's no crime in that. If you killed him, that's another story," Reese said in his calming voice he usually reserved for the victim's family.

He was so good at calming people down. Rory was usually good at riling people up.

"He was naked. Condom still on. Tie around his neck."

Reese coughed again, louder this time. Yeah, yeah. Rory would settle down and choose his words wisely from now on.

Ms. Cooper turned even paler, almost to the point of green as if she were about to throw up. Rory shouldn't have been so direct. He was starting to get the gut feeling she didn't kill the guy.

"I didn't...didn't kill him," she finally said after composing herself. She still looked green around the features as if one wrong word would send her running from the room to find a toilet.

"But you were there?" Reese asked in a soft voice.

"I feel like I should have a lawyer here."

"Only guilty people ask for a lawyer," Rory retorted, which made her flinch.

"What my partner meant is if you want a lawyer, we'll wait for one. We only want answers."

She nodded, then looked down at the table. "That's all I ever want. Answers."

"About your sister?" Reese asked.

She nodded again.

"You think Mr. Fontain had knowledge about your sister's disappearance?" Reese prodded.

"Yes." The one word barely left her lips.

It wasn't a confession, but it added to the evidence stacking against her. Not once had they given her the name of the dead man before Reese mentioned him.

"What exactly do you think he had to do with your sister's disappearance?" Rory knew he should've kept his mouth shut. Reese was getting more out of her than he was, but he couldn't. He was too intrigued now to stay out of it.

She looked up. "I don't think he had anything to do with it. But he had information to lead me to her."

"What do you mean by that?" Reese asked, frowning.

"I don't think she ran away like my parents think. Even the police think so. She never had a great relationship with our parents. They fought all the time. She challenged them at every corner. I won't disagree she left that day to run away. But she always called me when she got where she went. She didn't that time. I pressed the police, but they gave up before they even started. About a year ago, I swore I saw her. She didn't look herself. Her hair was blonde instead of brown and she looked...out of it. I don't know how to explain it. But when I called her name, she turned my way. Then some guy grabbed her and shoved her in a car. I've been working even harder to find her since then."

"What does that have to do with Mr. Fontain?"

Very good question. Reese asked it nicer than he would've.

"I can't be positive, but I think she's..." Ms. Cooper looked away, out toward the window.

"Ms. Cooper?" Reese said softly, coaxing her to keep going in a voice that always soothed people.

"Sex trafficking. I think my sister's stuck in that world.

Mr. Fontain is one of the men that keeps it going. Sick bastard." Her gaze flew to theirs. "I didn't kill him, though. I swear it. He was alive when I left. I didn't even sleep with him, although I might've given the impression I would. I did tie him up, but I left him alive once I got my answers."

"How did you find out Mr. Fontain was involved in that kind of business? What information did he provide you?"

"It's amazing what a person will do for someone they love." She looked away once again. "I work for an escort service. You'd be surprised by the kind of men that float around to different places. Sex can be a good motivator to get them to talk. I don't sleep with all of them if I get a weird feeling." Her eyes bulged as if she said the wrong thing. "Not that the escort service I work for is sex for hire. More like men hire us for dates and companionship. Sometimes, the moment turns intimate. But I don't get paid to have sex."

Reese nodded as if he understood. Rory chose to remain silent. They all knew the escort service's main point *was* sex. Whoever she worked for labeled it in a way to make it legal.

"My investigation led me to a few men who also get services from not so reputable places. Most wouldn't talk or give me much."

Rory wondered if the school knew about her extra job. Not that he was about to offer the information up to them. Ms. Cooper wanted to find her sister, believing her alive. He didn't exactly approve of her methods, but if no one else was helping her, what was she to do?

"And what did Mr. Fontain give you?" Reese asked.

She looked at Reese. "The location of a motel where he goes when wants a specific kind of woman. It's sickening. They can request by hair color, or body shape, how big their boobs are, eye color. They steal these girls and create an image for men to enjoy. My sister is stuck and I need to save her."

"What time were you with him? Anyone else join you two?" Rory asked, needing to get the images she created out of his mind. It *was* sick and disgusting. He could understand her intense need to find her sister and save her from that hell.

"I arrived at nine and left shortly after ten. He was alive when I left. And no, I was the only one there."

Based on the time of death, she left a few hours before he was killed. It didn't explain the second DNA found at the scene.

"You had no qualms about leaving a man tied up like that?" Rory asked.

"No." There was no remorse in her voice either.

"You said you might've given the impression you'd sleep with him. Did you put a condom on him?" Rory didn't want to ask, but they needed to develop some sort of timeline. Had someone else arrived after and found him like that and took advantage of the situation? Was she lying about everything?

Rory's gut said she wasn't.

"No, I did not. I tied him up with his wrists to the bedposts, but never went any farther. I started asking him questions then."

"And he answered them?" Reese asked, perplexed.

She looked down at the table. "Well, not without a bit of prompting to do so."

Ms. Cooper wasn't afraid of a bit of torture. Rory liked her a little more, although knew he shouldn't. She could've killed the man for all he knew.

"Can we have the name of the motel he gave you?" Reese asked. Then he smiled. "We'll help you find your sister so you don't have to go to such extremes. I'm sorry you ever had to."

A slow smile filtered onto her face, appreciating Reese's sympathy.

Rory felt for her. But if she killed the man, he'd lock her up so fast, she wouldn't see it coming.

BROOKE HAD DEBATED way too long this morning about showing up for work. The annoying meows coming from Willow and the chance people would look at her as if she were guilty helped make up her mind. Although she had been ten minutes late, nobody said anything to her about it.

Actually, nobody said much to her in general. She didn't think it was because they thought she was guilty. A morose atmosphere floated around the office. Nobody had liked Mr. Fontain. But knowing someone you worked with day in and day out had been murdered was hard to deal with.

Mr. Compton stopped in, informing her to field calls for Mr. Fontain's clients and that someone new would be hired soon to take over his position. He had treated it as if the man had up and quit, not been murdered. Of course, she didn't say anything to that effect. She nodded and did as she was told.

But such odd behavior. She'd mention it to Rory later. Maybe Mr. Compton killed Mr. Fontain. Maybe he had found out Mr. Fontain had slept with his wife. Love could make people do such monstrous things. Of course, she had never been in love before. Not the drop to your knees, seeing stars in her eyes, nothing else matters kind of love.

Although her insides turned to jelly, her jaw dropped to the floor, and her body wanted to jump Rory, she wouldn't say she was in love with the man. It had only been a day. But it was the closest feeling she'd ever had.

Work, despite the dreary cloud hanging over everyone, flew by. She left at five ten to make up for the ten minutes she had been late. She had texted back and forth with Rory throughout the day. Mostly innocent stuff, except one text had her going to the bathroom to splash a bit of water on her face to cool down. He had a devious streak. Because putting into actual words how he wanted to kiss her tonight —and not on her lips—seemed so naughty. She had never dated anyone like him before.

Oh, boy, she couldn't wait for him to come over. She stopped by the store and bought a box of condoms, another bag of doughnuts—because she couldn't help herself—and a bag of treats for Willow. If she wanted some alone time with Rory, she'd have to bribe her cat to leave them alone.

Willow was on her the minute she walked inside, circling her feet, meowing as if she had left her alone for a week and not an eight-hour work shift.

"Settle your tush down. I bought salmon treats. Your favorite." She pulled it out of the shopping bag and shook it. That garnered a few more excited meows from her.

Brooke didn't wait to pour her a few, setting them near her dish of food and water. Filling up her food dish, she then put the remaining treats in the cupboard, away from Willow's claws. She'd tear open the bag if she had the chance. Then she put the box of condoms in her room right on the nightstand. Why play coy? They both wanted sex and sex they would have.

If, after having fantastic monkey sex, the weird, erratic feeling disappeared, then she'd know it was a scratch she needed to itch and not the crazy thing people called love.

She took a quick shower, feeling dirty the few times she

had walked into Mr. Fontain's office, even though he hadn't been there. His stuff was still there. That lingering smell from his disgusting cologne. Memories from his slimy hand on her ass. She hadn't been able to shake the slight feeling of his presence in the room.

Her hair was still wet and needed to be combed, but she changed into comfortable clothes, nothing too sexy—a pair of short shorts and a tank top—when the doorbell rang. Okay, maybe it was a little sexy. A little too revealing. She wore no bra and the tank top had a hard time holding her babies up. And the shorts were the shortest she owned, her butt cheeks practically falling out. Dinner could wait—whatever he was picking up on the way to her house. She could be the first thing on the menu.

She didn't look before opening the door. She wished she would've.

Ted stood on her doorstep. His eyes took her entire appearance in and she swore she could see him salivating for a taste. Yep. Not happening.

"What are you doing here, Ted?"

She had to snap her fingers before he tore his gaze away from her chest.

"I thought we could go out to dinner. Although, I am all for staying in tonight. I heard about your boss. I thought you could use a distraction."

Gross. If she wanted a distraction from losing the world's worst boss—even if he was brutally murdered—she'd ask Rory to distract her, not Ted.

"No, thanks. We broke up, remember?"

He leaned closer, yet she still held the door and started to shut it a bit to get him to understand she wasn't about to let him in. He took the hint and backed up.

"I thought we could talk about that over dinner."

He just didn't get it. What was so hard to understand? They were over.

"There's nothing to talk about. We broke up."

Before he could respond with more whining about getting back together, Willow strolled to the door and meowed.

Ted backed up another step. "It's that dumb cat's fault. You love her more than me."

Her hand tightened on the door at his abrupt change of attitude. Like Jekyll and Hyde. She had seen small parts of this side of him in the brief time they dated. It was one reason she ended it. She would not fall into a controlling relationship. She didn't have anyone in her life to help pull her out if she got stuck.

Parents dead. One aunt who she rarely spoke to—she wasn't nice anyway. A few co-workers she hung out with on occasion, but none she'd call actual friends. Besides dating here and there, she lived a rather sad, lonely life.

"You need to leave, Ted. We're over. Please don't call me or come again." Then for added effect, because she knew Willow scared him, "Or I'll sic Willow on you."

He took another step back as if the very thought frightened him. He bumped into something, took a step to the side, and turned around.

Brooke was never so happy to see someone in her life.

Rory stood there with a six-pack of beer and a bag from a local Chinese place not far from her place. His expression said he wasn't amused.

"Can I help you?" Ted had the audacity to ask.

"You can stay the hell away from Brooke, or I'll take the cuffs behind my back and slap them on your wrists. When a woman says no, it literally means no." There was no mistaking the wrath in Rory's voice. "And I won't be gentle about it either."

If she had been teetering on whether or not it was love swirling around inside, she knew now it definitely was. She loved this man and how hot he looked threatening someone on her behalf. What a hero.

"She asked me to come over."

She gasped at his audacity. She did not.

"I suppose you're going to tell me she asked you to come over yesterday as well." The venom spilled from Rory's lips as his hands fisted around the items he was holding.

A muscle ticked in Ted's cheek, yet he didn't respond. Brooke had almost forgotten about the doorbell ringing incident and how Rory had rushed to her defense. One moment after another he displayed how heroic he was. He barely knew her, yet he kept showing up as if he cared a little too much. She wouldn't complain one bit.

"You have less than five seconds before I drop this shit and arrest you for trespassing and harassment."

Ted gave her one last glance, then walked away before Rory made good on his word. She had no doubt Rory would've. The fury in his eyes was easy to read.

He stepped inside and nearly walked back out when Willow meowed.

"Oh, don't worry, I'm sure that was a thank you, not a get the hell out. She never liked Ted," Brooke said as she closed the door before he could escape. The last thing she wanted was for him to leave. He just got here, and she was wearing her skimpiest clothes for him. Too bad Ted had to witness it as well.

"Does she like any guy you've dated?"

Brooke almost didn't want to answer that question. She offered a hopeful smile as she said, "Not yet."

Rory set the six-pack and bag on the small table she had near the door with a vase of flowers. Then he looked her up and down. She enjoyed his appreciative glance way more than she had Ted's.

"You look..." He moved closer and pulled her into his arms. "A lot tastier than the food I bought."

She bit her bottom lip, the nerves suddenly attacking her. She had been dying for this all day. His hands on her, everywhere. His kisses. His soft touch. His blue, blue balls to turn—well, whatever color they turned when satisfied. Not that she actually thought they turned blue. Did they? She didn't think so, but she had never seen it, so maybe they did.

"Shh..." Rory whispered as he pressed his lips lightly to hers.

Oh, dear. He said that in a way as if she had said that out loud, which she wouldn't doubt. When she got nervous, things slipped out of her mouth.

"I missed you today," he said before snatching another kiss. "I waited all day for this. What I didn't expect was to see your ex-boyfriend. Does he do that often?"

"No, he usually calls. Do you think it could've been him yesterday?"

"It might've been." Rory picked her up, a sexy-as-sin grin appearing. "Enough about him. I'll be around now, so no need to worry. Let's take this upstairs."

Well, she had no issues with that. On either account. Although, she wasn't one for bossing around. She'd have to have a talk with him about that. Assuming she'd want him around all the time was very arrogant. But she already knew the kind of arrogance he carried. She'd see how the sex was and how she felt afterward and then make her choice.

"I'm not arrogant. I know what I want. And when I want something, I do everything to get it."

Oh, shit. She was talking her thoughts out loud again.

"And the sex will be amazing."

She giggled as he started up the stairs. "You say you're not arrogant. What was that?"

"Confidence. Way different from arrogance."

He shut the bedroom door with his foot—as best as he could with the frame broken—then set her on the bed and leaned over her.

"Willow won't like the door closed."

A seductive grin grew as his eyes trailed from her lips to her chest. "Do you want me to open the door? Because I will risk her claws if you don't want it closed."

Oh, yes, she loved this man. Willing to risk his balls to Willow's deathly claws if it made her happy.

"No, I was pointing it out she won't like it closed."

At the moment, Willow took the opportunity to scratch at the door.

"See."

"We'll open it as soon as I'm done with you." He pressed a kiss to her neck, then grabbed the strap to the tank top with his teeth and pulled it toward her shoulder.

The light, grazing touch set her body on fire. His hand on the other side pulled that strap down.

"You're not wearing a bra." Light, sweet kisses were pressed against the top of her breasts, making her ache for more. For him to touch her nipples and take a bite. Anything. His touch was beyond what she could've ever imagined.

"I'm not wearing any underwear either." Her eyes widened and her hands tightened on his back, almost mortified she said that.

But the heat and desire in his gaze said she didn't say anything wrong. Of course not. She wasn't used to being so open and daring with a man. Sex was sex. It wasn't anything fun and exciting.

Oh, boy, she had been missing out.

"I don't know how I left your house last night without having you," he said with a harsh breath.

Then he stood up and took off his suit jacket—black today. His gun strapped to his side came off next and landed on the nightstand, his badge and cuffs went next to the gun. His eyes paused briefly on the full box of condoms as a wide smile appeared. Then his shirt disappeared along with his shoes, pants, and boxers.

She held a hand to his chest when he started to cover her. "Oh, no. The socks have to go too."

"My socks? I can't keep them on?"

"Eww, no, that's weird. Take them off."

Rory chuckled before whipping his socks off, then covered her body with his. "Now where were we? Oh, yeah, I was going to devour you from head to toe."

Then his lips found a nipple and all thought flew from her mind.

Oh, the delicious things his mouth could do.

RORY DIDN'T KNOW where to start. The beautiful perfection lying before him was making it hard to concentrate—even with the adorable rambling that slipped from her lips. He didn't worry she'd ever hide anything from him. He didn't think it was possible for her. She said what was on her mind, even when she didn't realize she was doing it.

He cupped one breast while his mouth devoured the other one. Her sweet moans filled the room, letting him know she liked it. His other hand slid down until it reached the top of her shorts. Then it slipped inside and sweet wetness hit his fingers. Oh, how he loved not having to contend with underwear. He didn't even want to mess with shorts.

He pulled his hand out, while his lips kept placing kiss after kiss above, to pull down her shorts. She helped kick them off and his hand went back to his prize until it found the spot that made her squirm and moan.

Her hands slid up and down his back, a bit through his hair. He continued to rub, coaxing delightful moan after moan from her lips. One finger, then two slipped inside her, rubbing, pushing, and hoping she let loose soon. He wanted to hear her come apart. Scream his name.

His lips made their way back up her neck to her ear where he took little nibbles, then ran his tongue across her skin. She trembled in his arms, clinging to him as the passion soared through the room. He was dying to get inside her, but not until she came apart first.

Her hands brushed through his hair as he hit the spot. She grabbed the ends of his hair and pulled—hard—as she moaned his name softly. Not exactly the scream he was looking for, but he'd take it. Even the sharp pain as it rattled down his spine.

He peppered a few more kisses across her cheek and her lips before removing her tank top completely. His mouth took a rosy nipple, his tongue swirling around, playing and getting to know it as if he had all the time in the world. And he did. He had no plans of leaving, not even when they finished eating and the sun set. He was spending the night and she'd have to deal with it.

Call it arrogance—she would.

He'd call it protecting her. Someone had to be around if

Ted decided to make another visit. That was his excuse and he was sticking to it.

He pulled away and reached for a condom. "Scoot up some."

"So demanding. Please, Brooke. Thank you, Brooke," she said with a silly grin but did scoot until she was in the middle of the bed.

Yeah, okay, he had a tendency to bark orders instead of asking nicely. Even Dr. Everly had nailed him about it yesterday. He figured he could work a little harder to use polite words, especially with her.

He tore open the condom package with his teeth, grinning like the devil. "Thank you, Brooke. You're right where I want you." Then he rolled on the condom, staring into her pleasured eyes as he did.

She watched him as he stroked himself, the desire increasing. It was hot as hell and he wanted to keep playing with himself while she touched herself. Well, later they'd have some fun with that. Right now, he needed to be inside her.

He had never felt this intense need to fill someone so completely. To be as close as possible to another person. He wanted to love her body, hold her close, and never let go. The feeling was intense and frightening. He chose to ignore it as he positioned himself and sunk deep inside her with one swift move.

She moaned in bliss and wrapped her legs around his waist, her hands and nails digging into his back as if she needed to get as close as possible to him as well.

"Hold on, sweetheart. I can't go slow." Then he grinned and added, "Please."

Their lips met as he started to thrust with vigor. Hard and deep, without restraint. He pounded into her as if he had to win a race and if he slowed down, he'd lose. She held on for the ride, clinging to him, never letting go.

He felt sweat trickle down his back, he was exerting so much strength in loving her thoroughly. Thrust after thrust. Filling her so completely, he knew he'd never be able to walk away from her.

The feeling of love swept through him so quickly, so desperately, he almost pulled out and scrambled off the bed. He had never felt this way before. It was frightening as hell. But he kept thrusting, hard and fast, refusing to let the powerful feeling scare him away.

"Deeper, Rory. Oh, please," Brooke murmured in a quiet plea.

Oh, she wanted deeper, he'd give it to her. And deeper he went, thrusting harder, almost afraid he might hurt her. Yet, the way she clung to him said he wasn't. He wasn't an asshole when it came to sex, but he took care to make sure he didn't hurt a woman. But her continued whispered pleas said she was loving every thrust as much as he was.

She was perfect for him. Absolutely perfect.

After thinking he'd never find love again—that he'd even want love again—hope sprang forth that he'd found the woman he was meant for. He only had to say a small prayer she felt the same way.

She cried out, digging her nails into his back this time when she came. Oh, the pain, yet he endured, pumping a few more times, hard and deep, before joining her.

His breathing was heavy as he pressed his head against her pillow. Then he twisted his head to kiss her neck a few times.

"I lo—" Whoa. What was he about to say? He couldn't say he loved her. They were only on day two of knowing each other. He didn't generally jump into bed with a woman this fast. Considering she never slept with Ted with three months of dating, he didn't think she did either.

Whatever was between them was not one-sided. It was intense and beautiful, but he had to tread carefully. The last thing he wanted to do was scare her away—and himself.

"You what?" she whispered breathlessly.

"I love you wearing almost nothing. Please do that more often," he said with a chuckle, hoping to dispel the sudden awkwardness he might've created.

She giggled, pressing her head into his neck. "You smell divine. I suppose I can do that, but only because you said please."

She seemed too good to be true.

He pressed a kiss to her lips, before winking. "Let's eat, then make use of some more condoms."

The sweet smile that drifted his away was enough to erase the fear coursing through his veins.

He loved this woman and he was jumping all in, no matter the consequences.

7

"So her cat literally ruined your shoes?" Reese asked as if he didn't believe him.

That damn cat was definitely a demon spawn from hell.

"Scratch marks all over them. It's like it's trying to tell me something."

Reese laughed. "Yeah, she's telling you to get the hell out of her house. I mean, geez. It's like you moved in. It's only been a week."

Best week of his life. He wouldn't deny Reese's words either. He had practically moved in. From their first time together in bed, he stayed the night. Now he had his own little spot in her closet, his toothbrush, shaving cream, and shaver in her bathroom, and his favorite granola bars in the pantry. His friend fixed the doorframe a few days ago, and everything was perfect.

He wasn't leaving anytime soon. Brooke hadn't given the indication she minded. While he had never moved this fast with a woman, it felt right with her.

But he had to find even ground with Willow. Because if the cat didn't start to warm up to him, he would be a goner sooner or later. If the cat didn't like you, you were booted out. At least, that was the impression he got from the stories Brooke told him, especially about past boyfriends.

It's not like he didn't try to get Willow on his side. He snuck her treats in the morning, right before Brooke came in to feed her and give her the actual treats she was supposed to have. Damn cat never said thank you. Usually stuck up her tail as if flicking him off and walked away as if she knew the game she was playing.

This morning, even after he had given her the treats, he found claw marks in his nice dress shoes. They were not salvageable. Not even a nice clean would help. He either had to live with it or buy new shoes.

What cat ruined shoes? It was dogs that ruined shoes.

"No comment?"

"Was I supposed to comment?"

"You've moved in," Reese reiterated as if he didn't hear him the first time.

"Not officially. So I've been spending the night...every night. It doesn't mean I've moved in. Plus," he said, shifting in his chair, "I don't trust her ex. He hasn't tried to speak to her since I said something to him, or tried to call her, but I've seen his truck drive by a few times in her neighborhood. I don't like it. I don't trust him. I'd rather be with her."

That was the excuse—a very good one, he might add— he was sticking with.

"No record on him. There's no history to suggest he'll hurt her."

Rory threw him a death glare. "Violent assholes have to start somewhere, don't they? You're telling me I shouldn't worry?"

"Well," Reese started, "I didn't say that. Just...make sure you know what you're doing. You're moving kind of fast."

"You were the one who told me last week to start giving a woman a chance. That's what I'm doing."

"Yeah, ask her out on a date. Not move in with her within a week. Dawn call recently?"

"Not since the last time I spoke to her. I guess me telling her I wouldn't be her sugar daddy in between guys didn't sit well with her. I can still hear her screaming in my ear when I said it."

Reese chuckled. "Too bad you married her. What were you thinking?"

"Thanks, man. Appreciate the support."

"Well, you got out in the nick of time before she cleaned you dry."

"Moving this conversation along. Think this raid will go well tonight."

"Sure hope so. It'd be nice to find Starla's sister."

Rory leaned back and swiveled his chair back and forth. "Starla? Since when are we on a first-name basis?"

"Since...right now. Excuse me. It'd be nice to find Ms. Cooper's sister."

"I agree. It'd be nice to close that case—not that it's our case."

Somehow, after speaking to Ms. Cooper, they had talked to the sex crimes unit about all the information she had supplied them. They were always on the lookout for things that might be considered sex trafficking in the city. It was a lot more common than the average citizen realized. It happened everywhere, in large cities, rural towns. With Ms. Cooper's information from the unfortunate Mr. Fontain— who they didn't think she killed—they were able to set up surveillance on the motel. Several different women were seen coming and going, along with different men, at all hours of the day. Tonight, they planned to nab the man who always transported the woman. Each woman was usually dropped off via a non-descript vehicle—never the same vehicle—and then returned a few hours later to pick her up. Each time they tried to follow the vehicle, they lost it. The person knew they were being followed and took protective measures to never be caught.

When Reese asked to be in on the raid yesterday, Rory couldn't help but speak up, too. If his partner would be there, so would he.

"Well, it's semi-related to our case."

Rory cocked a contemplative brow. "Are we thinking one of the traffickers offed Mr. Fontain? Because if they knew he gave up the motel location, then they wouldn't keep sending their women there."

"Don't know. It's a possibility. Or maybe he pissed off the wrong person. Digging through his life this past week has not shown us one person who liked him. I'm sorry your girlfriend even worked for him."

Girlfriend. He liked the sound of that. After his nasty ex, he didn't think he ever would.

"Me, too. Can't say I'm sorry the guy is dead."

At this point, it could be a man or woman who killed him. Dr. Everly confirmed after the autopsy he had died by asphyxiation. Although no DNA was present on or around the condom, indicating he never had sex with anyone. Ms. Cooper had been telling the truth about that. Which meant someone came inside his house, found Mr. Fontain already tied up, and made it look like he had sex by placing the condom on him. Why? What was the reason for making it look like something it wasn't? Dr. Everly had been right in a sense. The scene had been staged. If only they could match the DNA found on the tie, then they'd have their killer.

"Does Brooke know you won't be there tonight?"

"Oh, I'm going to her house afterward."

Reese's brows rose. "It could be like two in the morning. We have no idea when they'll show up at the motel. They show up at all hours."

"So?"

"She gave you a key already, did she?" Reese asked with a laugh.

"Well...no." Shit. He never thought about that. What would she say if he asked for one?

No, too soon. Even he knew he couldn't ask for a house key. It was one thing to bring over clothes and his toothbrush; it was another to ask for a key. He could demand one. It would play into his arrogance she said he loved to display. He wouldn't say he loved to do it; it was just a part of his personality. Plus, he liked to call it confidence, not arrogance.

"Looks like you'll be sleeping in *your* bed tonight."

"Shut up." Then he picked up his phone and sent a text, wondering if he wasn't a bit too arrogant like she suggested.

———

Gotta work late tonight on a case. I'll swing by to grab a key from you so I don't wake you up knocking on the door. Miss you.

BROOKE STARTED to chew on her thumb nail as she read the text again. A key? He wanted a house key.

She never said anything when he brought an overnight bag because, well, he had spent the night. Then she found more clothes hanging up in her closet. His toothbrush in her bathroom. His shaver on the sink, little pieces of hair in the sink. Ugh, he could at least clean it out after shaving.

Now he wanted a key. No asking either. The arrogance.

Yet, she didn't see herself not giving him the key when he stopped by. While it was a bit fast, a bit forceful on his part, she liked having him around. Even though Willow grumbled about it more than she cared to admit. For once, she loved a guy and she didn't want to give him up because her cat never liked any of the guys.

Not that she'd make it easy on him. She'd make him work for the key tonight. A few kisses. A few touches. Some hot sex against the front door.

Then she'd give him the key. Seemed only fair.

And she wouldn't respond to the text. Let him stew on that. He needed to learn that she didn't jump at commands. She might give in, but she wouldn't do so immediately. She had never liked to be bossed around. Stemmed from the fact her aunt was always telling her to do this and do that and never asking nicely.

At age sixteen, when her parents died, she had no choice but to live with her stern, bitter aunt who never wore clothes that showed an ounce of skin and thought fornication was the devil's work. She wasn't a nice person, to put it lightly.

She never let Brooke wear her hair up in a ponytail— showed too much neck. She couldn't wear tank tops or shirts that showed her neckline. No skirts, no shorts, not even sandals. What could go wrong looking at someone's toes? She couldn't hang out with friends after that. One, because they'd tease her at her new clothes. Two, because her aunt wouldn't even let her.

So started her new life of solitude. The few friends she had, she lost. When she graduated and moved out as soon as she could, she never made the effort to reconnect. It was as if those two years with her aunt had wrapped her in a shell that she was afraid to crawl out of. Oh, she ventured out here and there, dating guys who weren't right for her. Hanging out with a few co-workers so she wouldn't feel completely lame. But she knew she could do better.

She had taken the first step in becoming stronger and sure of herself by ending things with Ted. Normally, the guy dumped her because they couldn't handle her weird tendencies—or Willow. But with Ted, she had been the aggressor. Telling him no more. Plus, she had two years of someone controlling her; she wasn't about to let another person take the job.

The day rolled by at a snail's pace with no other texts from Rory. She wasn't sure how to take that. That he knew she wasn't happy with his demand, or that he found nothing wrong with her silence.

When she got home, she found her spare key and on a whim, shoved it inside her bra. He wanted her key, he could search for it. She smiled at her cleverness.

She fed Willow and rolled her eyes when she whined for treats.

"You know better. Once in the morning. Once at night." She started to open the fridge to look for something for supper when she pointed at Willow with a stern finger. "I know you clawed up Rory's shoes, too. I heard him swearing about it this morning, but he didn't tattle on you. You shouldn't even get a treat tonight for that behavior. Naughty kitty."

Willow meowed as if saying whatever, turned around with her tail high in the air, and walked away.

Such attitude from a cat.

She pulled some chicken out and decided she'd have chicken fajitas tonight. Rory walked in as she was cutting the raw chicken into slices. The audacity of the man. He didn't even knock. To be fair, she always left the door unlocked for him knowing he'd walk right in.

"That is how you cut meat?" he asked with muffled laughter as if he were trying hard to hold it in.

She didn't glance at her hands that were covered in yellow kitchen gloves, all the way past the elbows. Yes, she knew it was odd, but she didn't care. The texture of raw meat made her stomach crawl. Wearing the gloves helped to calm the roiling of her stomach contents as she cooked.

"Shouldn't you have knocked?"

"Shouldn't you have locked the door if you didn't want me to walk in?" Then his eyes narrowed as the concern mixed in. "You should lock your door."

"Then how would you get in?" She couldn't hold back her sly smile.

He came closer and rested his hip against the counter. "With the key you're going to give me."

"Gosh, and you asked so nicely, too."

"I thought I did."

Oh, she could drown in his sultry gaze and sexy smile. Yet, just because he had potent sexual power didn't mean she could let him get away with everything.

"You demanded. Not asked." Then she went back to slicing her chicken into fajita strips.

"Does that mean you're not going to give me a key?" The question came out a little more leery than she had heard from him before. Almost as if he were nervous she wouldn't give him one.

How would he react if she told him a flat-out no?

Did he even know what giving a key to someone signified?

Well, he had to. A person didn't demand a key and not realize the significance of it.

"I'll be late tonight. I don't know how late. We're doing a raid and it could—"

"A raid!" The knife slammed down hard onto the chicken, nearly hitting her finger.

"Okay, give me the knife. You can't be trusted." Then he nudged her on the hip and took the knife from her hand before she could argue.

She wasn't going to argue. She was still reeling from his words. A raid didn't sound good. It sounded very, very dangerous. Like bullets could start flying kind of dangerous.

"Go wash your hands, sweetheart. I'll finish cutting."

"Don't tell me what to do," she pouted, then walked to the sink and flung off her gloves, throwing them into the garbage can underneath the sink. She washed her hands vigorously with soap and water, scrubbing as hard as she could.

She ignored the fact she had indeed listened to him and washed her hands.

"Do you always throw away the gloves?"

Apparently, he was smart enough to ignore it as well.

"Eww, gross. I'm not touching them when they have meat guts on them. Yes, I always throw them away."

She was wiping her hands dry when he joined her near the sink, washing his own hands. He dried his hands, then grabbed her wrist when she started to walk away.

"I'll be okay, I promise."

Her gaze went from his hand wrapped firmly around her wrist, but not tight enough where she'd have to yank if she wanted to break free. She wasn't sure whether she wanted to break free yet. Then she drew her eyes to his honey-hazel gaze that was filled with too much worry.

"You shouldn't make promises you can't keep. Anything could happen."

His hand slid until his fingers intertwined with hers. She knew she didn't want to break free from that. What a sweet gesture.

"You're right. I shouldn't, but I don't anticipate any serious problems. It's a simple raid."

"I imagine no raids are simple. Stop trying to downplay it for me."

"Do you want me to stay home? I'll stay home."

Home? Only a week together and he was already calling her house a home. It didn't surprise her because it had only been a week—which it should've for that reason. No, it was because of the things he had told her about his ex-wife. She had heard the pain and the distrust in his voice as if starting another relationship so soon hadn't been in his plans. That trusting another woman was something he never imagined doing again. Yet, he was calling this home.

Well, she had trust issues as well. Ted had shown her not all men understand the words 'get lost.' Her parents deserting her at a young age—not that they could help it. Death didn't have an expiration date, it sort of happened. And her aunt, devil incarnate, for sure.

But home had a nice ring to it. Not just her and Willow occupying it.

"Brooke, sweetheart? Do you want—"

Yep. She wanted, all right. Her lips attacked his. This time she pulled her hand away so she could grab his head and guide him even closer.

He didn't hesitate to keep it going. He picked her up, her legs wrapping around his waist, and started walking out of the kitchen. When her back hit the corner of the wall leading out of the kitchen, he inched his mouth away. It didn't hurt too much as he hadn't been walking that fast, but there was a slight pain in her back.

She started to laugh because she had no good words. He joined her, then twisted them so she was flat against the wall in the hallway. Then his lips were back on hers and everything was perfect in her world once again.

This was what she had wanted. Even before he arrived. To make him work for the key and search her from head to toe, not that he even knew he was supposed to be looking for the key.

"You should go," she said between the powerful kisses that were sending her insides to mush and aching for more.

"So you're okay with me going?" he murmured, his hands trying to slide lower.

"It's your job." Her hand accidentally touched his gun when she had meant to try and weave a hand in between them to get to his zipper.

He chuckled, drawing the kiss to a close and setting her down. The pouty face she gave him garnered another chuckle.

"I should go."

"Or," she said, popping open his button and lowering the zipper, "you should stay for five more minutes." Then her hand snuck inside his pants and grabbed his cock that was hard and ready for her.

"Oh, sweetheart, I—" He cut off his words, a crease building between his brows, before taking his gun off his belt.

What an odd look, but whatever. She took that as her cue this was happening. Shoving her pants down and off, she barely waited for him to open a condom and slip it on before jumping up. He was her hero, like usual, and caught her. Then he was sinking deep inside, and she knew this was what heaven had to be like.

Happiness, laughter, and damn good sex all the time.

His lips found hers once again as he rocked her against the wall. Deep, hard thrusts the way she liked it. The kiss grew hotter and more intense as he pounded into her. She had never had sex like this before. Sure, they had fun in the shower and on her couch, but never against the wall or other piece of odd furniture. She loved it.

It felt so naughty and so not like her.

He shifted his hips, thrusting with abandon, making her moan between kisses as every spot he hit was such a good one. She could feel the bliss rising. When she felt his thrusts get a tiny bit more focused, yet deep, she knew he was close as well.

She came first, biting his bottom lip a little and grabbing a handful of his hair. He growled—whether in pain or ecstasy, she wasn't sure—then he pumped hard two more times before stiffening.

"Oh, yeah, this raid will be easy and simple. I'll be back for more of that." He pressed light kisses across her cheek and down her neck.

"You didn't even take off my shirt or bra."

His eyes twinkled with merriment. "I will not forget that tonight."

"Well, you should take a peek before you leave." She smoothed her tongue across her bottom lip, adding a bit of extra enticement for him.

He took the cue like a puppy in training. His fingers skimmed the top of her breasts, then a little lower as they slipped inside her bra. His eyes widened, then he pulled out the key.

"So, you were planning this all along?" he asked with the desire blazing in his gaze.

"Well, next time, I won't give you the hint to take a peek.

And try not to be too late." Then she kissed him hard before pushing on his chest to let her go.

He let her down gently and twitched when he glanced to his left. Brooke followed his gaze. Willow sat in the middle of the hallway staring at them.

"That's not creepy at all," he drawled, picking up his gun from the floor.

"She didn't meow or claw your balls, so there's that."

Rory shivered, probably from the image, then laughed with her.

They both cleaned up and she walked him to the door, hating he had to leave, still not liking the sound of this raid he was going to. The word itself made her jittery as if something bad was going to happen.

"Don't worry. I'll be home later." Then he kissed her soundly on the lips and left.

Home.

Yep, she liked the sound of that word, especially when he said it.

8

———

"Gosh, I want to hate you right now," Reese whispered. They were sitting in a van parked across the street from the motel with two other detectives from the sex crimes unit.

"Why is that?"

"You look like you had some fun before getting here."

Rory couldn't hold back his smile. Because, oh, boy, did he have some fun. Every time with Brooke felt like the first time. Amazing and impossible it could feel so good. So decadent, like a piece of cake you only had on special occasions because it tasted so rich your body couldn't handle it all the time.

And she had given him a key, despite how he sort of demanded it. He should knock that behavior off. One of these days it might push her away.

"Brooke gave me a key to her house. I had fun convincing her she should do so."

Although, in truth, she had every intention of always giving it to him. It made his heart leap with joy she had.

He was one lucky bastard. How had he gotten so lucky? After such a raw deal with his ex, he never expected to find such happiness again. And so quickly. He should thank whoever had killed the pervert Mr. Fontain, otherwise, he would've never met Brooke. The world sure worked in mysterious ways.

"I want to hear the details, and then I don't." Reese shook his head as if he couldn't decide.

"Hallway. Wall. Hot sex. Put them together." He grinned like the devil, then closed his eyes as he pictured Brooke in all her beauty, moaning in throes of pleasure.

"I hate to admit it, but I'm jealous. I never had wall sex with Carrie."

Yeah, but Carrie had also been the most uptight woman Rory had ever met. He still wasn't sure why Reese had dated her for two years. Thank goodness he never married her. While Carrie had never cheated on Reese, she had never been as emotionally involved as Reese had wanted her to be. Plus, she hadn't wanted children, which was something Reese had always wanted. They weren't getting any younger. Reese had better find a good woman before he ran out of time.

"You two know this is a small van. We can hear everything you're saying," Todd, one of the other detectives said, as he stared at the monitor in front of him.

"Have you had wall sex, Todd?" Rory asked. Since he commented, he had no choice but to be dragged into the conversation.

"You'd blush at the kind of sex I've had," Todd replied with a wink.

Doug, the other detective, laughed. "Take what he says with a grain of salt. He loves telling stories."

"In other words, Doug hasn't had wall sex either. I don't feel so left out now," Reese said, as they all chuckled with him.

Todd suddenly sat up and hushed them with a wave of his hand. "We got something here."

Rory put Brooke to the back of his mind, although it was hard to do, and focused on the plan at hand.

They had already watched as a single man, early forties, had walked into room four, alone. No bags. That alerted them immediately. They had waited for three hours for that to happen. Then another twenty minutes before whatever perked up Todd.

On the screen they watched as a young woman—maybe in her twenties, it was hard to tell on the camera—got out of a small red car. She looked around before heading to room four, knocking once. The door opened and she disappeared inside.

The car pulled out of the parking lot and started heading toward the city. The motel was on the outskirts of town.

He heard someone crackle through the mics they were following the car. Hopefully, they didn't lose the bastard this time. If not, they'd have the woman.

Doug maneuvered around stuff until he was seated in the driver's seat and headed across the parking lot. Todd talked into his microphone piece, coordinating with the other cops ready to storm the lone room. They all exited the van without a sound. He and Reese held back while Doug and Todd took the lead. Four other cops were circling the back in case the guy made a run for it—or there were more people on the lookout than they were aware of.

Todd kicked in the door. Rory could only roll his eyes. It's as if he was trying to show off his strength and skills. He had to agree with Doug. Todd was telling tall tales.

They all went in guns drawn, shouting "police." The woman screamed, rolling off the man and dropping to the floor. The guy had nowhere to go, so he did the smart thing and held up his hands, naked as a jaybird lying in the middle of the bed.

Well, they caught them in the act. That was a plus. Now he had to hope they caught the guy in the car and this woman would talk. Sometimes, even when they were rescued, the victims weren't always cooperative. Sex traffickers used many means to lure their victims, to coerce them into doing the things they didn't want to do. Threatening family members, drugging them. This woman looked pale and a little too thin to Rory. Her eyes were a bit glazed, making him think she was high on something.

He handed her a bedsheet that had fallen off the bed and tried to offer a gentle smile. This was Reese's job, but he stood closer and he didn't like the fear in her eyes.

"Here. It's okay. You're safe now."

She took the sheet with shaky hands and covered herself, but she didn't say anything.

Doug took over, guiding the woman toward the bathroom. He assumed so she could put her clothes on. Rory didn't argue. This wasn't his and Reese's operation, nor something they worked on often. This was why he liked dead bodies. He didn't have to figure out the right words to say to someone. What was he supposed to say to a woman who was forced to have sex with another person?

Todd cuffed the man after letting him get some clothes on and dragged him to the back of a patrol car. They'd interview him soon. They all waited impatiently for word on the car. It came what felt like ages later when it had been only ten minutes. The car had evaded them. Just. Great.

That meant they'd have to get the woman to talk about where she came from. Where they held her.

Based on the way she hadn't said one word yet, Rory

didn't see that happening anytime soon. By the time she did, the traffickers would have moved the other women by then. Considering they had a picture of Starla's sister, they knew this woman wasn't her. For some reason, he could tell that bothered Reese—a lot.

Maybe the guy would have some good answers for them. They could only hope.

"It's NINE o'CLOCK. That's too early to go to bed, isn't it? Are we lame or what? I mean, Rory will wake me up when he gets home. Isn't that such a great word? Home. I love saying it. No, I love hearing it more." Brooke sighed and frowned when Willow stood up from her lap and jumped off the couch.

"Well, fine. I didn't want to hang out with you either."

She'd had her fajitas, which were delicious. She had even liked Rory's thin strips better than the ones she had cut. He'd be her official meat cutter from now on. It made the most sense. He cut better strips and he didn't mind touching raw meat. Win-win for her.

After supper, she had taken a bath to relax and get her mind off Rory and his raid. Ugh. It should be easy and simple. Yeah, right. Nothing in life was ever easy and simple. It sounded scary and insane. She preferred he be honest with her, not give her false platitudes.

The bath hadn't helped. Not even reading a book by her favorite author, Aurora Lockheart, helped.

She had grabbed the new bag of doughnuts and gorged on a few before settling on the sofa. Switching from channel to channel made her feel pathetic, but nothing looked good.

She wanted Rory home.

Not even Willow was offering her comfort. Jumping off her lap as if Brooke disgusted her. Whatever. She didn't want or need kitty cuddles right now.

She nearly jumped off the couch when a knock sounded on her door. Nobody knocked on her door this late. Sometimes, her neighbors stopped by for this or that, but never at nine o'clock at night. Rory had a key, so it couldn't be him.

Willow stood near the entryway as if waiting for her to answer the door so they could kick some ass. Well, Brooke wasn't in an ass-kicking mood. She wanted to curl up in bed and wait for Rory to get home.

She approached the door with trepid footsteps, although it was locked. Whoever was on the other side wouldn't be getting in unless she opened it. She peered through the peephole and frowned.

Ted.

The man just couldn't get a clue. She was too plain and boring—borderline crazy cat lady, even though she only had one cat. Why was he so fixated on her?

To open the door or not open the door?

Meow.

She looked at Willow. Really? She thought she should open it. Willow did love hissing at him.

He knocked again.

Well, she wouldn't open it unarmed. Rushing to her fireplace in the living room, she grabbed a poker and gripped it in her left hand as she unlocked the door. When she opened it, she hid her body half behind the door as she looked at Ted.

She had already turned on the porch light for Rory, yet the yellow glow surrounding Ted gave him a menacing vibe. The look in his eyes frightened her. A bit possessive with a hint of anger.

Her hand tightened around the poker, yet she didn't reveal it. No need to set the bear off if she didn't have to.

"What are you doing here?"

She thought she sounded very nice, but by the way he frowned, it obviously came out more annoyed than she intended. Willow meowed behind her. Hers was easy to decipher. It wasn't a friendly meow.

"I thought we could talk."

"We have nothing to talk about. I've told you several times, Ted. It's over. I'd appreciate it if you'd leave me alone."

"It's that cop, isn't it? He's making you say these things."

"Ted, I'm asking you for the last time to leave. Don't come here again."

His frown increased, making his features even more menacing than before. The hatred in his eyes frightened her. For Rory? For her?

Then it all disappeared as a smile formed. "Brooke, baby, we can work through this. I'm sorry for stopping by so late. I'll let you get some rest."

She watched as he turned around and headed for his truck, a weird pep in his step as if she had agreed to a date or something. The man was clearly unhinged.

She slammed the door shut and locked it, double-checking it several times before satisfied it was locked. Then she got ready for bed, bringing the poker with her. She put it on her nightstand. It stuck out like a sore thumb. Well, whatever. It was the best weapon she had handy. She didn't own a gun. She wouldn't even know how to use one. That's why she needed Rory here.

She had a hard time falling asleep. Every noise she heard made her tremble and jump as if Ted was back. A few times, she even got up and looked out the window facing toward the street. She never saw his truck, yet the creepy vibes he was near wouldn't dissipate.

She must've fallen asleep because she screamed, reaching for her poker when a hand touched her on the cheek.

"Whoa, Brooke!" Rory exclaimed as he dodged a blow from the poker. He pushed back on it, twisting her arm a bit.

She dropped the poker to the floor as Rory hit the light on his side of the bed.

"What was that about?" He pulled her closer, running a hand down her side as if soothing her.

Oh, she needed him to calm her down. Her heart was still racing, the adrenaline still coursing through her veins thinking she had to go into flight-or-fight mode.

"Brooke?" He brushed another hand across her skin, this time lightly on her cheek.

Her body still trembled. All she could think of was how different this would've been if it hadn't been Rory. He dodged the poker with ease. Ted would've as well. She'd be a sitting duck in that case.

"You need to talk to me."

"I thought you were...maybe Ted."

Funny how she couldn't find her words when he asked nicely what was going on, but the second he demanded in a forceful tone for her to speak, she obeyed. She hated being told what to do, yet at this moment, she needed it. Another shiver wracked her body.

His embrace tightened, his lips touching the side of her head. A heavy breath escaped from him.

"Why would you think that? Tell me everything."

A question with a demand. She could work with that.

"He stopped by tonight. He sounded...very unstable. He got pissed when I told him to leave, blaming you. He thinks you're making me say these things to him. I guess it unnerved me more than I thought."

Rory cupped her cheeks, his gaze intense. "You don't open the door to that man ever again. Do you hear me? Understand?"

She nodded.

"If he calls you, shows up, anything that gives you the wrong vibes, you call me. I don't give a shit what I'm doing. You call me. Got it?"

Her head bobbed again.

"God, you scared me. Don't scare me, Brooke." Then he was crushing her in his arms.

She didn't care. For the first time that night—since Ted's visit—she felt safe.

"Tomorrow morning, you get a restraining order."

She'd go tonight if she could. There would be no arguments on that account, even though he had said it as if it were written in stone. Again, not asking her—telling.

He really needed to work on his pleases and thank yous.

But for tonight, she'd let it all slide. Huddling closer in his arms, she let his warmth and protection wrap her in a safe cocoon.

She never wanted to leave his arms.

———

9

A RELIEVED SIGH let loose as he grabbed Brooke's hand and walked with her out of the courthouse, her restraining order in her other hand.

"We got lucky. We got Judge Chance. He's a stickler about dealing with assholes like Ted. Plus, he's the dad of a good friend of mine who happens to be a detective."

Rory knew the moment he made eye contact with Judge Chance, Brooke would get everything she asked for.

"Meaning some judges wouldn't help me out?"

He tossed his head back and forth as if contemplating. "Some would want more evidence to slap someone with an order. Ted hasn't exactly done anything to you."

Of course, this was why Rory wanted her to get the order, so he didn't have a chance to do anything to her. Like put his hands on her, hurt her somehow. But he was escalating. Constantly driving by her house—something he finally told her about so she could tell the judge. Showing up and demanding to let him in. Not understanding the word 'leave.' Annoying, but not against the law. Some people would say he wasn't a danger, but a man with a broken heart.

Rory wanted to beat the living shit out of Ted for even scaring Brooke. He had never seen someone so frightened before. The fear in her eyes when he turned on the light, even knowing it was him, had been immense. She had honestly thought Ted broke in and had touched her. The fact she went to bed with the poker was enough evidence for him to know she was scared of the guy.

He squeezed her hand when a light shiver rippled through her body at his words. Adding more fear to her mind wasn't his intention, but he was being honest. He would always be honest with her, even if it wasn't what she wanted to hear. After his ex-wife putting him through the wringer with her lies, he never wanted dishonesty between him and someone else again. Once was more than enough.

He stopped her at the bottom of the courthouse steps. "Look, this is just a piece of paper. It doesn't mean he'll listen." He brought her hand to his lips when another shiver touched her, kissing it, telling her with that simple kiss he wouldn't let anything happen to her. "I don't say this to frighten you. I say it because it's the truth. We don't know what he might do, but maybe this will finally give him a clue that you mean it when you say you're done with him."

A low groan escaped when another tremble hit her body. All he was doing was scaring the living shit out of her and it wasn't his intention at all. He should shut up.

"If you even see him drive by you, you call the cops. I'm not messing around with this asshole. It's going to be okay. I promise."

He didn't have it in him to shut up. He had to make sure she understood the seriousness of this. Being with her twenty-four seven wasn't plausible, so he had to make sure she kept herself safe and made the right choices. Odds were, if she saw him driving, he was following her.

"Making promises again..."

He pulled her closer and kissed her. "That is one promise I will keep. No matter what."

"Hey, Rory."

He looked behind Brooke's shoulder, twisting her a bit as he still held her hand so her back wasn't to Ben.

"How's it going?"

"Good. Stopped by to get a warrant for a case Zeke and I were working on. You?" Ben glanced at Brooke and smiled.

Rory felt a small amount of tension leave her body. Part of him was annoyed one simple smile from Ben helped reduce her tension when he was holding her hand and giving her kisses. His touch should do more than Ben's dumb smile.

Laughter filtered into Ben's eyes as if he knew why the sudden frown hit his features.

"This is Brooke. My girlfriend." Rory made sure to emphasize the word girlfriend, even though he knew Ben was happily married. "We were getting a restraining order against her ex-boyfriend. We got Judge Chance."

"Good to hear. You should've gotten everything you wanted then. Sorry to hear that, Brooke." Ben offered her another smile, then held out his hand. "I'm Ben. I work with Rory. He has no manners introducing me."

Brooke chuckled and shook his hand. "He's always forgetting please and thank you, too. I get it."

"Excuse me. I'm standing right here."

Seriously. If he didn't know Ben loved his wife very much, he'd think he was flirting with his girlfriend. *His.*

"I hope you don't let him get away with that crap. He

needs to be put in his place now and again," Ben replied to Brooke with a wink as if Rory hadn't said anything at all.

"Oh, yes. Willow does, too. She doesn't play around with that. Manners are important."

This was getting ridiculous. Both of them were ignoring him.

"Good for your friends. My wife's friends are the same. They don't let me get away with anything."

Brooke chuckled. Rory couldn't help but laugh himself.

"Willow is her cat," he said dryly. "She's a demon spawn from hell."

"Hey," Brooke said, shoving her elbow into his stomach. "I can't believe you said that."

"Sweetheart, I adore Willow. She's my favorite cat ever." Then he kissed her, hoping to dispel the strange glint in her eyes.

At least, she didn't look completely pissed.

Ben snickered, enjoying the byplay.

"I apologized for what she did to your shoes."

"Your shoes?" Ben asked, still half-chuckling.

Rory rolled his eyes and lifted a foot. He had yet to buy new shoes. Ben's eyes widened, and then he started laughing harder.

"We've been thinking about getting a dog. Glad we're not thinking of getting a cat."

"Oh, dogs are worse. They'll chew right through it." Brooke smiled, the beauty of it lighting up her entire features and filling his heart with joy. "But I'm sure you'll be very happy with a dog."

He swore he had never felt this happy before, even when she was jabbing him in the stomach with her elbow, or her dumb cat was scratching up his shoes.

"Yeah, Corrine will love it. My daughter," Ben added when Brooke looked confused.

"Oh, I'm sure she will. Willow does a nice job standing in for what friends might do. She's very good at telling Rory what's up."

Brooke laughed, but Rory heard the awkwardness in it. Probably because she was realizing she was talking about a cat in lieu of friends. He didn't mind she didn't have many friends. It meant he didn't have to contend with anyone else when it came to Brooke's time.

"I bet. He needs it," Ben replied with his own awkward chuckle.

"Still standing here," Rory muttered.

"Hey, what are you two doing tonight? We're having game night at my house. You're welcome to come." The kindness in Ben's eyes told Rory he wasn't saying it to make Brooke feel better about her lack of friends.

Ben was just a nice guy like that. He'd hung out with him and Zeke, a few other detectives now and again, but he didn't make it a regular thing. He hung out with Reese most of the time, and when he was married, he had been forced to hang out with Dawn's annoying friends. Yeah, he didn't miss that.

"We'd like that. Thanks. What time?" Rory replied when Brooke didn't say anything.

"Eight o'clock. No need to bring anything. We'll have drinks and snacks. I'll see you tonight."

Then Ben was off and they were headed back to his car so he could drop her off at work and head to work himself.

"He only invited us because he felt sorry for me." The sadness in her voice couldn't be mistaken as she shuffled into her seat and shut the door.

He grabbed her hand, kissing the top of it. "We don't have to go if you don't want to."

She held his gaze a moment. "We can't back out now. We should go or I'll be late to work."

Then she looked ahead, although didn't pull her hand away. But the way she had torn her gaze from his felt like she had pulled away from him.

It hurt. Nicked his heart a bit.

Nobody felt sorry for her. Definitely not him. Not Ben, either. Ben was being nice.

Not wanting to argue, he let it go. He could only hope she didn't continue to pull away from him.

His heart wouldn't survive it.

"I CAN'T BELIEVE we're doing this. He only said it because he felt sorry for me."

Rory pulled her hand up to his mouth and pressed a kiss to it.

Brooke swore her heart melted more and more every time he did that. It was one of his favorite things to do, especially when she was upset. She wouldn't complain. She adored the gesture. It didn't take away from the fact that she was right about Ben, though. He had felt sorry for her.

No friends. Talked about her cat as if she were one. How much more pathetic could she get?

She was a crazy cat lady—with only one cat.

"He said it because he meant it. Ben's one of the nicest guys I know. Come on. We'll have fun. These guys always used to get together on Fridays for drinks, but now that they're all married and have kids, they changed it to game night. I've heard Ben and Zeke talk about some of their wild game nights. I'm excited to be a part of it for once. But don't tell them I said that. I'll deny it."

She giggled at his silly look, yet knew he was being serious.

Rory laid another tender kiss to the top of her hand before pulling her toward the front door. It opened before they could knock.

"Oh, sorry, dude. Excuse us."

Then two teenagers holding skateboards walked past them and dashed off the porch steps. A woman with bright-pink hair appeared in the doorway.

"You be back in two hours. No negotiations, Adam. I mean it this time."

"Yeah, got it," one of the boys yelled with a hand in the air, yet didn't look behind him. She assumed that had to be Adam.

"Hi. I'm Mel. Come on in." She held the door open wider for them.

"Oh, Ben's wife. Nice to meet you."

Mel made a funny face and laughed. "Oh, gosh, no. That would be Rina. I'm with Newman. He's the sexiest one in the room. It's easy to pick him out." Mel winked at Rory as if Brooke wasn't part of the joke or something.

She felt so out of her depth. She didn't know any of these people, and they all knew each other. She'd stick out like a sore thumb.

"Hey, glad you could make it, man," another person she didn't know said as he shook hands with Rory.

"Yeah, me, too. This is Brooke." Rory squeezed her hand. "Brooke, this is Zeke, Ben's partner."

"And the better of the two," Zeke said with a grin as he shook her hand. "Nice to meet you, Brooke. Sorry you got stuck with this joker."

Brooke laughed, not sure how to respond. They were all very easygoing with each other, and she always became awkward and weird around people she didn't know.

"What he meant to say is you're the luckiest woman here," Rory replied when she didn't say a word.

"Come on, Brooke," Mel said, looping her arm through hers as if they were the best of friends. "Let's leave both of *these* jokers alone."

Then Mel pulled her, giving her no choice but to let go of Rory. He offered a smile but didn't stop the woman she didn't even know from bringing her into a dining room full of more women she didn't know.

Mel introduced her to everyone. Zoe was married to Zeke with one child, Zabrina, who was one month shy of turning three, and another on the way. Rina was, of course, married to Ben, with one child, Corrine, eighteen months old. Dee, who Brooke found very loud, was married to Sauer, who she was told was very quiet, the exact opposite of Dee. They had one child, Brock, who was fourteen and a half months old. Mel, of course, was married to Newman. Adam was her fourteen-year-old brother she had custody of, although didn't venture into the reason why. Susan, the last woman to be introduced, was married to Stitch. No kids and none on the agenda yet. Out of all the men, she wanted to meet Stitch the most, just based on his name, and ask why he was called that.

Rina poured her a glass of white wine after asking her preference, and then they all took a seat around the table. Brooke wondered if the games involved alcohol as the table was filled with different bottles of wine and liquor. There was also a plate of cheese and crackers amongst the bottles.

"So, Brooke, how'd you meet Rory? He's always so

serious and stone-faced. Very d...irect man," Dee said as she primped her hair.

Brooke had a feeling Dee wanted to call him something else but changed her mind at the last second. By the few giggles and furtive glances around the table, the others knew what she had wanted to say.

Yep. She totally felt out of place.

She took a large gulp of wine before answering. "My asshole boss was murdered. He showed up to question me because I called out sick, and I guess that made me look suspicious. But Willow gave me an alibi because, of course, I didn't kill him, even though he grabbed my ass when he shouldn't have and he was such an asshole. Then Willow clawed his balls and he left. Then I called him because a knock scared me, and then he kissed me, and then it's like he practically moved in. I gave him a key and he didn't even ask. My ex keeps showing up, and I got a restraining order today and met Ben, and here we are."

Five sets of eyes stared at her.

She took another large gulp of wine, finishing the entire glass.

Yep. So out of her depth.

"So, what game are we playing tonight? I'm terrible at games." She should keep her mouth shut. Or leave. That sounded like a good idea, too.

Dee grabbed the wine bottle in the middle of the table and filled up Brooke's glass with a devious grin. Brooke wasn't afraid to admit it scared her.

"Don't be scared of us. We're all friends here," Dee said cheerfully.

Oh, dear. She was saying her thoughts out loud again.

"Let's start with Willow. I love a woman that will claw a

man's balls. She sounds awesome," Dee said with a chuckle as she primped her curly red hair once again.

"She's my cat." Brooke took another sip of wine.

Oh, she was *so* a crazy cat lady.

"I almost adopted a cat the other day working this one crime scene." Susan made a pouty face. "Stitch wasn't a fan of the idea. Don't tell him this story, Brooke. He'll never warm up to the idea." Then Susan laughed, a nice friendly one as if trying to break her tension.

Because Brooke was sure she was the only one who felt the odd, awkward tension circling the table.

"Yeah, not all cats are like that. Willow's always had such sass since I got her." She took another sip of wine. No more gulps. Sips only, or she'd be confessing her whole life story before the games even started.

"Relax, Brooke. Like Dee said, we're all friends. Even you. You're dating a cop now. It's not easy being a cop's wife —or PI," Zoe said with a wink to Mel, giving Brook the impression Newman was a PI, not a cop.

"Or the opposite," Susan added. "I work in the crime lab. Stitch is a tattoo artist. He doesn't always have it easy. I can work weird hours and some of the scenes are...disturbing."

"So, you should be with the guys, and Stitch should be here with us." Dee slapped the table with a laugh as if it were the best idea ever.

"He'd never come to these things if I even remotely suggested that," Susan said with a bit of horror on her face. "It's hard enough to get him here."

"What everyone is trying to say is you're welcome here. No need to be nervous. We've all dealt with a bit of...craziness before." Rina blushed as she continued to speak in a soft voice. "I'm talking about your boss being murdered. That's how Zoe met Zeke first."

Dee cleared her throat. "Not exactly how she first met him."

Zoe threw a napkin at Dee. "Let's not get into that."

"Anyway," Rina said, "welcome to our group. We don't always play games at these get-togethers. Tonight, all the kids are with our parents, so we're putting the games to the side so we can drink and chat and relax."

"She's our voice of reason if you couldn't tell," Dee said with a smirk in Rina's direction.

"And she's the one with no filter," Rina retorted with a sweet smirk.

"And I'm the crazy cat lady who says everything she shouldn't." Despite the nerves still flowing rampantly through her, they were making her feel more at ease. Brooke liked these women.

Maybe she'd have friends for once.

Real friends.

Ones who would understand, like Zoe said, dating a cop. She still couldn't make the worry leave from the raid Rory participated in.

"Well, I'm all for hearing more about your cat clawing Rory's balls." Dee snickered.

"I almost want to grab a notepad and pencil. This is good stuff to use in a story," Mel said. "I mean, if you don't mind."

"Story?" Brooke asked as she lifted her glass for another sip.

"Oh, you don't know. Mel is a writer. Meet Aurora Lockheart."

Instead of swallowing, the wine spewed from her mouth.

All over the table.

If that didn't say how pathetic and idiotic she was, she didn't know what would.

RORY TRIED to look toward the dining room, which was half-hidden by a wall. All he could hear was laughter, so he could only assume things were going well. As long as they weren't laughing at Brooke.

No. Those women wouldn't do that to her. He'd met them all before. Parties here and there. He only had to hope they were making her feel welcome and not making her the butt of their jokes.

"Chill, man. She's good," Newman said quietly next to him as another conversation was going on with the other guys. "Amelia was nervous the first time meeting everyone, too. They're all making her feel welcome. I have no doubt. The only one I'd worry about is Dee."

Sauer backhanded Newman on the shoulder, indicating he had been listening to both conversations. "Don't say that about my wife."

Newman cocked a brow. "You know your wife."

"She's honest, but not cruel," Sauer countered.

"So, this is game night?" Rory asked, hoping to dispel his nerves because these two weren't helping like they thought they were.

"Sometimes we just have drinks and convo. Kids are with the grandparents, so we're forgoing the games tonight." Newman took a sip of his beer. "I always lose when we play games, especially charades, so I'm not too sad."

"How's the business going?" Rory was curious. Not that he'd ever quit his job and become a PI. He knew why Newman had because of everything that went down when one of his ex-lovers was murdered and he had become a suspect for a short time.

Not that Newman was missed by everyone at the

precinct. He had burned bridges before he left. Rory didn't mind the guy. Newman never pissed him off, so no hard feelings.

Newman smiled. "Picking up speed. It's doing well." He frowned. "A few hiccups. I had a new guy a month or so ago..." Newman blew out a breath. "He had just started working for me. Former deputy up north in Lucky. He was looking for a change. A missing person landed in my lap and it happened to be a girl from up in his neck of the woods. He found her and a bunch of other women in a sex trafficking case."

"That's great news." Rory didn't see where the hiccups came in. Newman could have some insight into the recent sex trafficking case they had landed in.

The guy had gotten away, and the girl wasn't talking. She was too frightened. For all they knew, all the other women had already been moved to a new location, so even if she did start talking, they wouldn't get much. They could hope, though.

"Yeah," Newman said regrettably, "he was murdered shortly after by a gang. Unrelated, but sometimes I wonder if I hadn't sent him back up there if he might still be alive. He had wanted to get away from the area."

"You can't beat yourself up about it," Sauer said, clapping him on the shoulder in support. "It wasn't your fault. The way Logan talked about it, that gang has been after them for a while now."

"Logan?" Rory inquired.

"Local sheriff up there. Also Derek, the guy who was murdered, he was his best friend." Newman produced a smile. "Shit, enough of the depressing stuff. How'd you meet, Brooke?"

"Still depressing convo," Rory said with a laugh. "Her boss was murdered. I suspected her of it until I met her."

"Sort of like Zeke," Newman said with a chuckle.

"Hey," Zeke interjected, obviously hearing his name. "I never suspected Zoe of murder."

"No, but you thought she was a prostitute," Rory countered.

Everyone laughed, even Zeke.

"Any leads on the case?" Ben asked.

Rory shook his head. "Not one. He had a lot of enemies. Real douche, as Sauer's wife would say."

Sauer chuckled and nodded, knowing how Dee loved to call men that wonderful word. Rory had no doubt he was on that list of hers. Most men were.

"How'd the raid go?" Zeke asked.

He relayed everything, even the part where the woman wouldn't talk. "Any tips, Newman?"

Newman shrugged. "I wasn't involved in that part. Derek called the local authorities once he found her and the other girls. They took over. My case was closed. I can't imagine what those girls go through. It can't be easy to talk about."

"Well, I keep hoping and praying she talks soon. The woman who was the last to see my dead guy alive, her sister is missing. She thinks she's trapped in that world. Reese has, like, made it his mission to find her sister for her."

"She off the guy?" Stitch asked, finally joining the conversation.

Rory shook his head. "Don't think so. I believe her when she said she left him alive, tied up to the bed." He couldn't help but laugh.

When a woman got one over on an asshole like that, it was funny. Not funny he got murdered shortly after, but still.

"Let us know if you need help," Zeke said with a chuckle. As if insinuating he and Reese couldn't handle it.

"Won't need it." He took a sip of his beer to hold back a retort he shouldn't dish out.

"So, this crazy ex Brooke has. What's up with him? Let us know if you need us to help out with that." Ben held up his hand before Rory could interrupt more offers of help. "I mean, like if you have to work late and you want someone to be with Brooke and stuff. I know how hard it is to worry about someone you care about and work at the same time."

"Yeah, maybe. I appreciate it."

Then he ran down everything about Ted and how Brooke had been taking it. Not well. He still couldn't get her swinging that poker and the fear in her eyes out of his head.

"Ted Calhone?" Ben asked, sitting up a little after Rory finished speaking.

"Yep. You know him?"

Ben nodded. "He's a personal trainer at Pump It Up Fitness. I've never had him, but I've seen him there. He looks weird at the women. He's always given me bad vibes. I'll talk to Dickens about him. He owns the place."

Rory tipped his bottle in thanks. "I'd appreciate that. Report back to me what he says." Then Brooke's smooth voice appeared in his mind. "Please and thank you."

"Whoa, Brooke's rubbing off on you." Zeke laughed and everyone joined him. Even Rory.

She was.

He wasn't one bit sorry about it.

10

"I FEEL SO SILLY. But thanks for coming." Brooke had to force the giddiness in her voice to settle down.

Her favorite author was walking inside her house. Seriously. This couldn't be real.

Mel giggled as she reached down and petted Willow on the back, which made Brooke think she said her thoughts out loud again. Whoops. Willow's quiet purrs filled the foyer, telling Mel she liked it and wanted more.

"What was Rory talking about? She's adorable and oh so friendly," Mel said as she gave Willow some more scratches behind the ear and on her neck.

Brooke shut the door and chuckled. "Well, he wasn't exaggerating. She's not a fan of guys. I have wine." That came out more awkward than Brooke intended. She was terrible in social situations. Especially when she was nervous, and oh boy, she was nervous.

Her favorite author!

The soothing laughter that filled the room from Mel helped her nerves calm some.

"I would love some wine. I'm happy to be here. I never

get out of the house." Mel rolled her eyes as she followed Brooke toward the kitchen. "By choice. Adam has me running around with so many school activities and whatnot, which is great he's getting involved, but I like being a homebody."

Brooke poured them a glass of white wine. They took a seat at her dining room table where all five books she owned by Aurora Lockheart sat with a pen ready for her signature.

"Me, too. Peopling is hard."

More laughter filled the room.

"You speak my language." Mel took a sip of wine, then grabbed the books. "I can't believe you own all these."

"Are you kidding? I'm not just saying it when I say you're my favorite author. My favorite. Like, I could re-read them all the time. I appreciate you signing them." This time Brooke rolled her eyes. "And whatever Rory told you and Newman, it's not like I need a babysitter. I know he's working late tonight, but I have a restraining order. I don't think Ted's dumb enough to break it."

Mel paused with the first book open and the pen ready. "Don't underestimate people." Then she smirked with glee filling her eyes. "Plus, let the guys act all macho and like they're your hero. They can't help themselves, and it gives them a sense of control when, really, they know we're the bosses. And I don't mind girl time. I rarely get out like this. Sure, I get together with the other ladies, but sometimes, it can be..." Mel tossed her head back and forth. "A lot."

Brooke nodded. She enjoyed herself a few nights ago at the so-called game night. Drinking, laughing, and hanging out with other women was nice for once. But she understood what Mel was trying to say. Those other women didn't hold back. They talked about everything and anything. At one point, Dee had even said, "What's said at the table, stays at the table." Then she regaled a story about her and Sauer and sex in the bathtub. Brooke almost covered her ears because she wasn't used to such openness. Although, now she was tempted to try the position with Rory. Girl night wasn't all bad with the women.

Mel signed all five books for her, and Brooke knew she'd never touch them again to read. She'd have to buy a different collection for her to read. These books were sacred now. Signed by her favorite author. Eek!

"You make me feel good right now, and I'm not talking about the wine," Mel said with her own giddy smile. "It's always nice to hear people like your books."

"Love. I *love* them," Brooke said as she stood up and grabbed the wine from the counter and transferred it to the table.

"More?" she asked as she poured more in hers, but didn't want to be presumptuous about Mel's.

Mel nodded. "Newman's picking me up later, so don't mind if I do."

Brooke couldn't believe she drank the first glass so fast, but she did. She wouldn't mind drinking the entire bottle itself.

"Did he have plans?"

"Not really. He's working a few cases, but he usually tries to do most of that during the day. He was going to drop Adam off at Nicholas's, Ben's nephew. They've been best friends since we moved here. Can't get them apart. But I'm grateful. Adam had a hard time connecting with other kids when we lived up north. I'm glad he made a friend here. He's spending the night so I don't have a curfew."

Brooke cheered to that when Mel raised her glass.

"How did you come about raising your brother?" She put a hand over her mouth. "That was so forward. Forget I asked."

Mel waved a frivolous hand in the air. "Doesn't bother me. I'm an open book. Most people get weird around me and how candid I can be. My dad was an abusive asshole. My mom finally got fed up and defended herself for once and killed him. She's in prison."

Oh.

Dear.

Brooke took a large gulp of wine. She hadn't expected *that* story, nor how easy it came out of Mel, even though she had said she could be candid.

"That's. Wow. I'm sorry your mom's stuck there. That sucks."

Mel twisted her lips in a way that said she wasn't sure whether if she wanted to laugh or cry. "It does suck. You're one of the few to be real about it. Most people don't know what to say. I've been trying to get her out and fight it, but I don't think it's going to happen. But, until then, Adam's stuck with me, and we're making it work."

Willow took that opportunity to jump up on the table and sashay in front of them as if she owned the joint. Which Brooke wouldn't dispute. Half the time she did rule the house. Even Rory capitulated to her demands. Jumping on his lap, eyeing him until he gingerly petted her. Brooke thought he did in fear she'd claw his balls again if he didn't. Then, other times, she hissed at him as if he were pond scum. A person never knew what kind of mood Willow would be in. Tonight, she wanted to be part of the conversation.

Willow plopped down in the middle and rolled so her belly was on display as if saying, "Rub my belly, bitches."

Mel giggled, then proceeded to do just that. "You're awesome, Brooke."

She slammed a hand to her mouth. "Did I say that out loud? That is such a terrible habit."

"Well, to be fair," Mel said, "Willow did plop down with that expression. It fit."

Their glasses emptied quickly again. Brooke refilled them.

"Should we order pizza or something? I have frozen lasagna I can toss in the oven. I should've been more prepared for this."

Although, she had been prepared for the most important thing. Her books getting signed. The wine. Everything else sort of slipped her mind.

"Pizza sounds good."

Brooke ordered two medium pizzas with extra-cheesy garlic sticks, then grabbed another bottle of wine.

"You read my mind," Mel said with merry laughter as she finished the rest of her glass.

"This is nice. I like this."

Brooke loved it, actually. Hanging out with another woman. Doing girl things with someone other than an animal. Wow. It's sad how pathetic she was before meeting Rory.

"Not pathetic, just different. You were being you and there's nothing wrong with that."

This time, instead of brandishing a hand to her mouth for saying her thoughts out loud again, she shrugged, rolling with it. It wasn't nerves making her do it. Because Mel had an easy way about her, making her not nervous at all. It had to be the alcohol. She was consuming a lot of it, and she didn't imbibe very often. A glass here or there, but that was it.

"So, weddings. You got married in October. I imagine a fall wedding would be so lovely."

Mel's eyes got large. "It was a nightmare. His mother is..." Mel took a gulp this time. "She wanted everything to be perfect, and I was to the point I would've been game to go to the courthouse like Sauer and Dee had done. Newman stepped in and told his mother to settle her shit down. I would've, but, you know, it's his mother."

"I can't even imagine. Instead of bridezilla, it was mother-in-lawzilla. That's not a thing. Forget I said that. I love your hair. It's so pink and so cool." The wine was messing with her head. She couldn't even stay on one topic for long. Plus, wedding talk had turned into a disaster. Mel probably didn't want to talk about her crazy in-laws.

Mel ran a hand through it, smiling, loving the compliment. "It's so fun to do."

"I would never be brave enough to do it."

"Sure, you could. You'd look great with it."

With her mousy brown hair, she didn't think so.

She scrunched her nose up as if disagreeing.

"I have the best idea," Mel said as she slapped an excited hand to the table.

Willow jumped and raced off the table from the sudden noise. Brooke didn't even care, she was so focused on the excitement in Mel's gaze.

"Something that we shouldn't do because we've had two going on three glasses of wine."

"No, it's an amazing idea."

Oh, this new Brooke. The one that hung out with other people for once. The one that had an amazing, sexy boyfriend. The one that wasn't going to let an asshole ex keep frightening her. She was ready for amazing.

"Let's do it."

Whatever *it* was.

RORY ROLLED OVER, expecting to meet a soft body, and felt nothing but semi-cool sheets. He popped open his eyes to see Brooke not in bed. Although she couldn't have gotten out that long ago as her spot wasn't completely cold.

He grinned when he heard a sharp curse word echo from the bathroom. So she was up and getting ready for work. Bummer.

He had worked later than he anticipated last night on a new case that had landed in his and Reese's lap. He had been about to walk out for the day when the captain called them, throwing a new case at them like they weren't already swamped. He had been sorry when he had to tell Brooke the news. Then he had suggested she call Mel to hang out, get her books signed.

Oh, he knew she saw right through it. He didn't want her home alone right now with the restraining order still fresh and new. He didn't trust Ted.

She didn't argue—much. He could've asked her nicely to do it instead of telling her she had to. He couldn't help himself. Barking orders came naturally to him. Why ask when he needed something done regardless? It didn't help his dad had been in the military and he grew up with his old man telling him what to do every single day. Obviously, he rubbed off on him.

But he would try harder, especially with Brooke. Things were going so smoothly with them, he didn't want anything to ruin it.

When he got home last night, she had already been in bed. Not surprising considering the funny text he got from

Newman, telling him he had picked up a very drunk Mel. The ladies had a good time together. That's all Rory cared about. He had undressed, slipped into bed without turning the lights on so he didn't disturb her, and fell asleep.

Glancing at the clock, he groaned. He wouldn't even have time to properly love her this morning. She wasn't a fan of being late, and if he did what he wanted to do with her, she'd be late. He didn't have to go in for another few hours, considering he got home so late.

He sat up and got out of bed, deciding it wouldn't hurt if she was a few minutes late. What was so wrong with a few minutes?

He rounded the bed when the bathroom door opened. Brooke walked out. He stopped in his tracks.

"Your hair..." His mouth dropped open a bit. "Is blue."

She absently combed the bottom portion of her hair as a tentative smile crept out. "It looks terrible, doesn't it?"

Well, no, it didn't. Her entire head wasn't blue, only the bottom tips of her hair as if she had let someone dunk her bottom half into a bowl filled with blue liquid. Although, it wasn't a straight line all around either. It flowed in an easy pattern. It worked well. Her eyes were a brilliant green, and with the splash of blue, it made her eyes sparkle even more with elegance.

"You're gorgeous. It looks wonderful on you." He laughed. "I didn't expect to see you with blue hair."

She bit her bottom lip as her smile started to expand. "Well, Mel and I might've had quite a bit to drink. One talk led to another and yeah. This happened."

He walked closer and grabbed her hands, raising them with an aching patience to press a tender kiss to each one.

"It looks lovely." And that was not a word he used—ever.

But it was the appropriate word because she did. "Why'd you pick blue? Favorite color?"

Because these were things he needed to know for the future. Birthday, anniversary, and any other important date where he might need to buy her a gift.

"Oh, no, I love yellow." Her lips twisted with mischief. "I got blue because...well, we were talking about...you know...umm...girl stuff."

He cocked a brow, not following. "Girl stuff?"

She nodded vigorously. "Yeah, stories and such."

"Stories and such?"

"Your blue balls," she blurted, then started to giggle until a snort came out. "I had too much to drink last night."

He joined in her laughter, then kissed her deeply. "Blue balls. Good one."

She pulled one hand away from his and patted his chest. "I better get going. I hate being late."

He whined, adding his best pout he owned, yet it didn't sway her. She gave him one more kiss before dashing out of the room, looking sexy with her new hairstyle, and her clothes matching. A light-blue cardigan with a white blouse, black pants, and the cutest blue high heels. Not that he described shoes as cute—ever—but on Brooke, it looked cute.

Deciding it would be useless to crawl back into bed—he was wide awake now—he took a quick shower and got ready for work. He jumped a little when he walked into the kitchen and found Willow sitting on the counter, staring. Hard. At him. Like she had been waiting for him patiently to walk in and scare him.

"Looking for your secret treat, are you? I spoil you, yet you still have an attitude most of the time with me. What I do have to do here, cat? Beg on my knees for you to like me?" Rory swore Willow smirked as if yes, he would have to do that.

He rolled his eyes and placed three small treats in front of her.

Meow.

"So demanding. Please and thank you go a long way, so I'm told." Then he dropped another two treats by her feet.

Grabbing a quick breakfast, he had to force himself to ignore Willow's meows as he moved around the kitchen. He was not going to give in with more treats. Brooke would spank his ass for giving her what he already had. Not that he'd mind a little spanking.

But better to not wake the beast, so to speak.

"Be good." He pointed at Willow as he tossed on his suit jacket near the front door. "No parties or having friends over. If you see Ted, claw his balls until they fall off."

Willow responded by turning around and waving her tail in the air as she did so. He'd take that as a big 'get the hell out.'

And he was losing his mind anyway. He was talking to a cat like it was a human being. Like a kid he was leaving home alone unsupervised. Like Brooke talked to her.

Geez, Brooke was rubbing off on him more than he realized.

He was at work for an hour before Reese rolled into the building. They weren't making much headway on their new case, nor was the case involving Brooke's boss going anywhere either.

Digging into the man's life proved he pissed off way too many people. Owed money to some unsavory people. Slept with too many married mens' wives. Terrible person to work with. It was easier finding people who liked him—nobody.

According to Brooke, nobody seemed to miss him at

work. She already had a new boss, overtaking Mr. Fontain's position as if he had never even worked there.

While he wasn't sorry the guy was dead—he had treated Brooke with so much disrespect, he would've loved to beat the shit out of him—he liked to close his cases. It bugged him they couldn't close this one. Hell, it bugged him they didn't even have a small lead. There were too many possibilities.

"Wanna grab some lunch then find a witness?" Reese said, indicating the new case they were working on.

He nodded, threw on his jacket, and headed outside. "I'll drive."

As they neared his car, his steps slowed. Fury started to bubble to the surface.

Reese paused on his side. "What's up?"

"Someone keyed my damn car!" He couldn't do anything but stand there and stare, the anger building with intensity.

Reese rounded the vehicle and whistled low. "Damn."

The marks were deep, extending from the driver's door to the gas tank. Two long rows of scratches that would cost him a pretty penny to get fixed.

He wasn't a huge car fanatic like some guys were, but he took care of his car. He kept it clean, got it washed, made sure to keep it maintenanced. What pissed him off the most was someone had the audacity to even come at him like this.

He turned around and headed back to the building.

"Where you going?" Reese shouted, yet Rory could hear he was following him.

"Check the surveillance cameras."

He had to smooth talk Becky, the officer in charge of security around the building. There were protocols and procedures to follow in order to look at the security tapes.

Rory didn't give a damn about any of that. He wanted to know who touched his car.

"There," Reese pointed as Becky stopped the video, rewound it a bit.

They watched a person wearing a hood covering their features well walk by his car one way, then swivel sharply—still blocking their face—and walk back again, dragging something across his car. Then the person walked away as if heading out of the parking lot and eventually out of view of the cameras.

"Keep looking."

Becky pursed her lips at his demanding tone, her eyes narrowing.

"Please," he added with a gentle smile.

Yeah, he really needed to work on his manners.

They searched through more of the videos but saw nothing else. What little they did have, they weren't able to tell who it might've been. Rory had no doubt it was a man. The height and build of the person had been stocky and tall.

While he hadn't had the best of conversations with Dawn a few weeks ago, he didn't think she'd stoop to something this low. Hell, they had been divorced for over six months. If she had wanted to get back at him, she would've done it then. And not with his car. She would've drained his life savings in any manner she could've. That was her specialty on screwing people over.

"Well, I think we have one suspect," Reese said casually, leaning against the desk. Becky shooed him away, not liking how he was so close to all the equipment.

"Yeah, I think you're right."

Because besides Dawn, the only other person he had issues with lately was Ted.

The bastard thought he could mess with a cop.
Not on his life.

11

"How about I do the talking?"

Rory cocked a brow, frowning. "How about you shut the hell up?"

Reese snickered, yet was wise enough not to say anything else. When he got pissed, watch out. His wrath could be brutal. Not that he meant to take it out on his best friend, but there was no way in hell he was going to stand back while Reese handled this.

No. Way. In. Hell.

This asshole was messing with the woman he loved, and now he thought he could mess with him.

It was a good thing he and Reese were so close because he knew Reese wouldn't let anyone speak to him the way Rory just had. And later, when he was calmer, he knew he'd apologize and ask for forgiveness. Right now, all he wanted was to smash in Ted's face.

He stopped at the counter at Pump It Up Fitness, and before he could say a word, the beefy guy behind the counter spoke.

"Welcome to Pump It Up. Where we will pump. You. Up.

I'm Dickens. The owner and best personal trainer you'll ever have. I don't recognize you gents. Not members. Let's turn that around."

A shiver rippled throughout Rory at the dude's scary smile. Like, so scary, he wouldn't hesitate to arm wrestle a pen into his hand and make him sign the paperwork. He felt Reese tremble as well.

"Nice pep talk. But not why we're here." He pulled his badge from his belt and slapped it on the counter. "Detective Walker. I'm here to see Ted Calhone. Now."

Dickens' smile dimmed, as if in slow motion. Like a movie fight scene. The frame slows down, the karate kick soars through the air and hits its target, blood spewing from the opponent's mouth, lips flapping, eyes rolling back. A person can see the pain. Feel it.

Yeah.

Right now was not the best time to be demanding and in-your-face with someone. Especially someone larger, with way more muscles, and definitely stronger than him. Rory had no problem admitting that Dickens would kick his ass.

He hadn't meant to offend Dickens. He just wanted Ted.

Ben had spoken to Dickens about Ted like he said he would, relaying to Rory the next day that Dickens didn't have much to report about the guy. Came to work on time. Friendly with his co-workers. No complaints against him by any clients. Clean as a whistle, as far as Dickens was concerned.

That report had not made Rory happy, but when Ben had suggested it, he hadn't expected much to happen.

"Detective Walker, did you say?" Dickens finally replied, as if he had to find his composure so he didn't beat the living shit out of Rory.

The man still looked upset. Of course, when he didn't

smile, it made his overall size and appearance look very menacing. Rory would prefer his cheesy-ass, sign-up-today smile over his frown.

"I did. You know my friend and colleague, Detective Stoyer."

A hint of a smile graced Dickens' face before disappearing. "Ah, yes. Ben is very good about keeping to his schedule here. I had a conversation the other day about Ted with him."

"He mentioned it to me."

Dickens pressed his lips together in a weird duck-like face, then smoothed them out. "Never had any official complaints against Ted. I was surprised and saddened to hear he's giving his ex a problem."

"Well, he's now extending that to me, and I'm not happy about it. I sure in the hell am not happy about him harassing Brooke. I'd like to speak to him." Rory refrained— just barely—from adding the word 'now' again.

You only poked a bear once. Well, only an idiot poked a bear at all.

"It's funny you're stopping by today asking for him. He came in this morning. He wasn't in a good mood. Hasn't been in one since he was served the restraining order. In the past three days, I've had several complaints against him from clients and co-workers. He's rude and surly, and last night, he even touched one of the women inappropriately. I fired him this morning as soon as he walked in. He's not here, detective."

Well, damn. Rory had not expected that. Ted was losing control. And a man recently dumped, refusing to leave his ex alone, harassing her like it'll change her mind, losing control was the last thing Rory needed.

Because he was bound to escalate his anger toward only one person—Brooke.

"What time was stamped on that video, Reese?" Because Rory was having a hard time focusing after Dickens' info dump.

"10:52 the hooded individual was first seen walking toward your car," Reese spit out like a human computer. His partner could store information in his head like a memory chip. It was scary sometimes how well he remembered things.

Rory offered a small grin toward Dickens, hoping to lessen the fury boiling inside. "What time did you fire Ted?"

"He arrived at 8:05, five minutes late. He walked out less than five minutes later after I watched him clean out his locker." Dickens finally produced a genuine smile. "I'd say that gave him plenty of time to do whatever he must've done to you. I'm sorry he's derailing."

"Derailing is an understatement," Reese muttered. "He could do anything. Got fired. Lost his girlfriend. She has a new boyfriend."

"Shit. I need to get to Brooke now."

He twisted around so fast, he almost hurt his neck when he jerked back toward Dickens. "Thank you. Sorry for the attitude."

"You can make it up to me by stopping back and signing up." Dickens' smile frightened Rory so much, he turned around and practically ran out of the building.

Sign up? Yeah, not a chance. Not with a guy like Dickens breathing down his neck.

He raced to his car, pulling out his phone as he did. He needed to hear Brooke's voice. He needed to know she was all right.

Her phone went to voicemail.

He tried again as he sped out of the parking lot.

"Slow down, dude."

Voicemail again.

If something had happened to Brooke, Ted was a dead man. Cop or not, he wasn't about to let anyone get away with hurting the woman he loved.

When he finally made it to Brooke's office downtown, his heart was racing a mile a minute, and his feet couldn't run fast enough. He even bypassed the elevator when it didn't immediately open when he pushed the button. He didn't even know if Reese followed him, his mind was so centered on finding Brooke.

As he pulled open the door to the fourth floor, he took a few deep breaths to attempt to calm himself down. The last thing he wanted to do was frighten Brooke even more than she was.

He opened the door to the advertising agency where she worked and flashed his badge at the receptionist. He didn't say anything or wait for her to ask him what he needed. He turned left and headed down the long hallway, her voice trailing behind him. Didn't care. Nothing was stopping him from getting to Brooke.

He took a right and finally breathed a sigh of relief when he saw her sitting at her desk, chatting away on the phone. The minute she saw him, she smiled, then ended her call abruptly.

Brooke stood up. "Hey, what are you doing—"

His lips cut off the rest as he pulled her into his arms. The kiss was hard, intense. All the anger, all his fear went into the kiss. She moaned, her hand curling into the front of his shirt. Yes. Oh, yes. He wanted her so badly, he could feel his cock jerking to attention. But that's not why he came here. That's not why he pulled her into his arms.

He had needed to feel her. Confirm with a touch that she was okay. That nothing bad had touched her. Only his touch.

Hating it, but knowing he had to, he slowed the kiss, then slowly disengaged his lips from hers.

"Wow. Okay. That was..." She frowned, yet he saw the desire still shimmering in her eyes. "What was that? What are you doing here?" Then she glanced behind his shoulder. "Hi, Reese. What are you doing here? Did something happen? Are you—"

Another kiss exploded between them. He couldn't help himself. Although he hadn't intended to, just by showing up —with Reese in tow—he had put a slice of fear into her. He heard it in her voice as she spit question after question out.

A throat cleared behind them.

Rory smiled against her lips, then pulled away. "He's no fun."

She giggled, then lost her happiness as she glanced at the two of them. "So, what's going on?"

"I missed you." Rory forced out a laugh, hating the lie that slipped out. But he didn't know where to begin with Ted. He didn't want to frighten her even more.

"You missed me?"

He leaned closer and whispered, "I wanted more than a kiss this morning, sweetheart. You left me hanging."

She slapped his chest playfully. "Oh, stop."

"Reese and I were going to grab lunch. We thought you'd like to join us. Right, Reese?" Rory looked at him, his brows rising and his eyes telling him what he couldn't say out loud.

"Yep. Lunch."

Smart man. Going with the flow.

"Oh, I'm sorry, Rory. I'm swamped. I don't think I can get free for lunch. Maybe another time."

He nodded. It had been a spur of the moment, how-do-I-continue-my-lie kind of thing anyway.

"Supper, then. I'll pick you up from work. I'll take you somewhere nice."

Even though he told himself to stop sounding so forceful and demanding, it came out exactly like that.

"Or I can drive home in my car," she said softly, yet narrowed her eyes, telling him he should've phrased it more as a question. "Are you sure there's not something going on?"

Yes, there was, which was why he would demand this. One last time.

"I'll pick you up. I'll be here at five. Don't leave."

Then he kissed her breathlessly one more time, leaving her dazed and ready to pick up where they left off at home.

Maybe tonight, he'd tell her about Ted.

Well, no maybe about that. He had to. She had to be safe.

Before he left this building, security would understand that if Ted so much as walked past outside the place, he was to be notified.

———

"HE WAS ALL like 'I'll pick you up. Don't leave.' Me, man. You, woman. You listen, is all I heard."

Mel burst out laughing, the sound so refreshing in her ear. Brooke had never had this type of friendship. One where she felt comfortable enough to call someone to tell them her woes. After fretting about Rory's visit for more than two hours, she finally caved in and called Mel. She was so glad she made the decision. Mel had such an art of putting her at ease.

"Girl, don't let him dictate everything. Plus, you're right. What about your car? Like, why is it so necessary he pick you up?"

"Thank you." Brooke slapped her hand on the desk, wondering the same thing. "He never said. He was acting in his usual arrogant way."

Usually, she let him get away with it. Sure, she voiced her displeasure, but she usually caved to his demands.

Well...not today.

"I'm driving home today."

"Yep."

Mel's immediate agreement made Brooke feel better.

"I can leave early from work." She rolled her eyes. "Well, like, fifteen minutes early. We're swamped. I can't leave too early."

Mel chuckled. "As long as you get out before he gets there, otherwise you're gonna have a caveman in your midst."

"Don't I know it? Maybe I'll sic Willow on him too when he gets home."

That garnered more brilliant laughter from Mel.

"Although, she might not cooperate. She looked at me funny this morning when I was getting ready for work. I think it was my hair."

"That looks absolutely amazing."

She wouldn't disagree. Despite being very drunk when she had it done—with Mel's stylist able to fit her in on such short notice—Brooke loved her new style. The pop of blue made her feel bold and daring, something she had never felt in her life. She lived in her little bubble, surrounded by a protective shell, and she never stepped out of it.

It was time she did.

She started with her hair.

She had been nervous this morning getting ready, hoping to get out of the house before Rory woke up. While she loved her hair, the worry had wormed its way inside people would hate it. Judge her for it. Maybe even tease her. Of course, it would've started with Rory if she wasn't quiet trying to escape the house. But he had been awake.

Thankfully, he had liked it. As long as he hadn't been lying to her. His behavior was odd, stopping at her work as he did. While his demanding ways were nothing new, she had the impression he was holding something back from her. Maybe he had also done the same thing this morning when complimenting her hair.

No. Rory wouldn't lie. Trust was important to him. He had said so when speaking about his ex-wife and the way she threw the trust out the window, cheating on him. Idiot woman. Rory had his odd tendencies, but he was a great catch. She felt lucky to have snagged him.

"You still there, Brooke?"

She shook her head of the negative thoughts, holding to the fact that Rory hadn't lied and he liked her hair.

"Yeah, sorry. I better go. It is busy here. I needed to vent a little. Thanks for being my sounding board."

"Anytime. Let's get together this weekend and get our nails done or something. I enjoyed last night."

Maybe she wasn't the only one craving friendship. It was nice to know she wasn't alone in the feeling.

"I would love that. It's a date."

Ugh. She was such an idiot. A date? They weren't in a relationship in that sense. She had made it awkward.

Yet, Mel didn't sound like it was weird. She repeated it was a date, told her to stay strong dealing with Rory, and hung up.

With Mel's encouragement and her not wanting to let

Rory think he could keep telling her what to do, she left fifteen minutes early like she wanted. Of course, her heart pounded and her hands turned all sweaty as she rode the elevator and walked to her car. The entire time she expected Rory to pop out of nowhere and start harping on her for not listening and that he refused to let her drive home.

But he didn't, and she made it to her car with no incidents. Twenty minutes later, she was home. Willow didn't greet her at the door, although she found her in the kitchen, sitting next to her empty bowl, staring at her. With her beady, judgy eyes as if saying, "Why haven't you fed me yet, peasant?"

Brooke rolled her eyes. "You know, you're as bossy as Rory. Honestly, you two are perfect for each other."

She stomped over to the container where she kept Willow's food. It made her feel better to stomp. The noise bugged Willow because she meowed. Or she was telling her to hurry up.

Either way, Brooke took her time because she would not be bossed around by a man—or a cat.

She tossed a quarter cup of food into her bowl, refilled her water bowl with fresh filtered water from the fridge—because Willow wouldn't drink anything else—and then ate two cookies before getting started on supper.

No more than thirty minutes passed before she heard the front door slam. Not a loud shove to close it, but a booming slam that filled the entire house.

Rory was home.

He found her in the kitchen tossing the chicken into a stir fry pan. She had a craving for Chicken Mei Fun. A fun recipe she discovered online that she had found rather easy to make. Not all recipes were the best when she tried them, but this one was on par.

"You left work early. Without me." His voice sounded strained as if he were trying very hard to hold in his anger.

If anyone should be angry, it was her. For being bossed around like a child.

"Oh, I managed to get everything done before the day ended. With how slammed we were, it was amazing I did. I thought I'd get an early start on supper." She flashed him a smile, then grabbed an onion to dice it up while the chicken cooked.

"You left without me."

She glanced up. "I don't like being told what to do. You didn't even ask, Rory."

She brought her attention back to the onion, refusing to believe her eyes were watering because he upset her. The onions were making her cry.

Warm arms circled her, then his hands covered hers. She hated to feel grateful when he gently took the knife from her hand. But she did because it had been shaking so much she would've cut herself. She always had a hard time holding in her emotions.

He started to dice the onion with her cocooned in his embrace. No tears emerged, but her eyes continued to feel watery and ready to explode like a waterfall any second.

"I'm sorry, Brooke. You're right. I didn't ask. I was..." He fell silent as he finished dicing the onion. Then he set the knife down and backed away, washing his hands at the sink.

Then he grabbed the spoon she'd been using to stir the chicken and tossed the pieces around some.

"Do the onions go in yet?" he asked as if the conversation was over.

"You were just, what?" She wasn't about to let him get off that easy.

He sighed, a crease building between his brows as he frowned.

"I was worried about you." He swallowed hard. "I'm worried about Ted hurting you."

But she had a protective order against him.

"Why? We took care of that."

Rory brushed a tender hand across her cheek. "It's a piece of paper. It doesn't mean he'll listen."

"So something did happen?"

He looked away, indicating she hit the nail on the head. "Someone keyed my car today. I don't have proof it's him, but I have no doubt it was. He was fired from his job today as well." He pressed a light kiss to her lips. "I'm worried. I'm sorry I sounded so harsh at your work. It wasn't my intention. I don't want to frighten you."

"Well, I'm a big girl. I can handle it. Next time, tell me the truth right away. Trust, remember?"

He answered with another kiss. Longer, deeper. Oh, yes, he remembered. This kiss was intense and powerful. He told her everything she needed to know from it.

He pulled away, but not enough where he couldn't dip in for another kiss if he wanted. "So, what's next with whatever we're cooking?"

"You're going to help?" she asked breathlessly, her eyes trailing to his lips. She wanted more kisses. More of everything when he touched her so desperately.

"Of course. I enjoy being with you, no matter what we're doing." Then his eyes trailed to her lips, shimmering with desire. His hand reached for the stove and flipped the burner off. "On second thought, let's eat after."

"Aft—"

Yet, she never managed to get her question out when he swooped her up into his arms. Instead of heading for the bedroom, he went to the living room, and Brooke didn't even care when Willow meowed at being booted from her spot on the couch.

Rory's touch scorched her body, wowed her soul, and made her feel like she was the most precious person on the planet.

Oh, yeah, supper could wait.

12

SKIPPING THE BREAD AISLE, where he knew the doughnuts were located, he headed for the snack aisle instead. Rory knew Brooke loved her sweets. Doughnuts, cookies, hell, he even found a Snickers stash in one of the drawers. While he wanted to make tonight special and show her he cared without actually saying the words, he wanted to try something new.

He paused halfway between his destination and the other aisle he knew would put a smile on her face. Maybe he should go the easy route.

After learning she didn't take well to his demands—leaving work before he got there and putting him in panic mode again—he still hadn't learned his lesson.

The next morning, he told her he'd bring her to and from work.

Asking would've helped his situation. Because she told him no, in no uncertain terms. No amount of begging had changed her mind. If he would've asked in the first place, he probably would've gotten the answer he wanted. So he *followed* her to work—and home from work.

Yeah, she hadn't been too happy with him when they got home.

Then this morning, he tried the asking route. She still denied him. Told him Ted hadn't done anything, and she didn't think he would. He was smarter than that.

Rory barely managed to not roll his eyes. Smart men still made very stupid mistakes, especially when they felt jilted. Jealousy and revenge could be dangerous.

So he followed her to work again.

The text she sent him wasn't pleasant.

Don't think I won't take your key away from you. Stop following me.

Although her text had ended there, he had envisioned the rest of the words she hadn't said. *You're acting like Ted.*

Which had made him pause and fret and worry all day that—well, yeah, he was acting a bit like Ted. In his defense, though, he was only following to make sure Ted didn't do anything to her. He didn't trust the guy.

But, after talking to Reese, who agreed with Brooke's assessment he should back off, Rory realized he had some damage control to do.

So, here he stood in the grocery store trying to think of the best I'm-sorry-for-acting-like-a-jackass treat—with flowers.

He swiveled, grabbed a bag of chocolate-covered doughnuts, knowing he had to go big or go home, then ventured to the snack aisle and grabbed popcorn as well. A set of red roses on his way out almost concluded everything he needed. He made a quick stop to the liquor store for the best bottle of wine he could find, then stopped and bought the sappiest, sweetest, romantic movie. At least, based on the description it sounded like it. He wouldn't know. Chick flicks were not his thing.

That last purchase pained him. A lot.

But Brooke loved chick flicks, and he loved Brooke. End of story.

It bothered him, terrifying tingles slithering down his spine, the horrifying images he conjured, but he drove home without stopping at Brooke's work.

She made it clear this morning she wouldn't tolerate him following her to and from work, even though it was because he cared. The last thing he wanted was her taking his key away and kicking him out.

He hadn't officially moved in, but he *had* moved in. He hadn't been back to his house, except to pick up a few items here and there. They should talk about that.

Or he needed to slow down.

Nope. They should have a talk about that. He didn't like the idea of slowing down. Brooke was the one. He felt it deep down in his bones. Dawn—she had been an anomaly. A point of reference of what not to fall for in a woman. A mistake that showed him what he truly wanted in a woman.

That woman was Brooke.

He arranged the roses in a vase he found in the top cupboard above her fridge, then placed them on the coffee table in the living room. Next to it, he put the movie, doughnuts, and the box of popcorn.

Willow jumped on the coffee table and circled the items.

"Hey, shoo!" He waved his hands at her, but she didn't budge. "Don't make a mess. Seriously. Did you think I'd forget you? I can't have you watching us have sex in the living room again. It's unnerving."

Meow.

"Well, don't do it if you don't like watching it." Then he

rolled his eyes, berating himself for talking to a dumb cat again.

"Here." He pulled a mouse toy filled with catnip out of the bag and tossed it toward the dining room. "Don't say I never think of you."

Willow raced after it without even saying thanks. Well, as long as she kept herself scarce while he loved Brooke once again on the couch.

The front door opened. At the angle he stood, he watched her walk inside, her expression serious and subdued.

Something happened.

Damn it.

He should've followed her like his instincts told him to.

"What happ—"

"Oh my, what—"

They both stopped speaking at the same time. He stared hard at her, trying to figure out how serious whatever it was that happened. Her eyes were glued to the things on the table.

He swept a careless gesture at the items. "I'm sorry for being a jackass—again."

A slow smile crept onto her face, calming his racing heart. He had overreacted. She simply had a long, exhausting day. He knew he did. Still no new evidence on Mr. Fontain's case. Still no new leads on the whereabouts of Starla's sister and the other women trapped by traffickers. Yeah, it had been a shitty, useless day.

He couldn't stand the distance anymore. Stalking to her in four long strides, he didn't miss a beat as he kissed her thoroughly, telling her what was soon to come.

"What a welcome home," she said with a chuckle, yet the humor was missing. It sounded flat and dull.

Something *was* wrong.

"You okay? What happened?"

"Nothing. Very uneventful day." Then she pointed toward the closed door. "Until I got home."

Ouch. So she didn't like his apology? She hadn't said thank you, or I forgive you.

"I don't know how else to say I'm sorry, okay. I'm trying here." He hadn't meant to snap at her, and he cringed inside when she pulled back a step.

"That's not what I meant. How long have you been home?"

He frowned. "Twenty minutes or so."

She grabbed his hand and pulled him toward the door. "Come."

He followed, confused by the way she was acting. When he walked outside with her and followed her gesture at his car, it all made sense.

"What the hell!"

He could only see the two tires on this side of the car were flat, but a walk around the other side confirmed those were flat as well. Someone slashed his tires.

Most likely Ted, the asshole. And he wouldn't be able to confirm it unless someone in the neighborhood saw. Brooke didn't have security cameras outside her property.

"You okay?" she asked softly, grabbing his hand again when he walked back to her side.

Okay? No, he was nowhere near okay. He wanted to shove cuffs on Ted, lock him up, and throw away the key. Yet, unless he proved it was Ted, he couldn't do a damn thing.

"I'm fine."

"You don't sound fine."

He turned his attention to her, pulled her hand to his lips, and pressed a tender kiss upon it. He might be upset, but he didn't want her to worry. Obviously, she did, if seeing this destruction and walking into the house with a morose expression said anything. Oh, it said everything. She was trying to be strong for him, yet these things scared her, and they weren't even happening to her. Why was Ted going after him?

Well, better him than Brooke. He could take the guy on and kick his ass until the sun didn't shine. Brooke wouldn't be able to do the same.

"I saw a movie on the table. What one did you get?"

He didn't want to change the subject, but he was grateful Brooke had. Because he didn't want this to ruin the evening he had planned for her. Derail it some, but not ruin it.

"Some cheesy chick flick I knew you'd enjoy. I don't remember the name."

"Very thoughtful of you. And apology accepted."

The smile that lit up her face—albeit small—calmed the fury building inside. He wouldn't let this ruin his night. That's what Ted had intended.

"Why don't you pop the popcorn, toss the pizza in the oven—it should be preheated by now—and I'll take care of this. I won't be long."

Hopefully, not too long. He'd call it in and pass it off to another officer to knock on doors and find a potential witness. Technically, he was the victim. It was the right thing to do.

Didn't mean he liked it.

———

SHE TURNED around from the oven and flinched, rolling her eyes at Willow, who sat on the counter staring at her.

"You're not getting any treats right now. Why are you on

the counter? You know I don't like that," Brooke chided her, then picked her up and set her down.

No matter how many times she pulled Willow off the counter, the sassy cat still jumped back up like it was her right. Brooke was the adult in this house. Willow was the cat. One wouldn't see that with the way Willow acted all the time.

She grabbed the popcorn and bottle of wine from the living room. The smile that hit her lips couldn't be wiped away.

It had been thoughtful of him to go through so much trouble. Doughnuts, a movie—and she knew he didn't like to sit and watch romantic comedies and such. But for her, he was willing, just to apologize.

Part of her wanted to apologize. Because although she had been firm in her text—way easier than speaking aloud —she had been nervous the entire drive home. How silly. She didn't think Ted would lash out at her. Yet, Rory's worry and concern had transferred to her, especially when she walked out of her building, got into her car, and noticed Rory not following her home. The fear had crept in. His worry increasing hers like a fire building in intensity. A small flame to a roaring blaze.

Then she got home and saw Rory's tires and...and she didn't know what to think. She had no doubt, like Rory, that it had to be Ted.

Yet, was it? Would Ted be that vile and aggressive because she wouldn't date him anymore? While he had been demanding—a bit like Rory, yet creepier about it—she hadn't sensed an underlying possessiveness about him.

Rory was a cop.

He dealt with bad guys all the time. It had to be related to one of his cases. Like the one with the woman and her missing sister. Rory didn't go into a lot of detail, but he had said Reese had made it his mission to help the woman find her sister. It was also the raid he had been a part of.

That made more sense someone bad from his case was messing with him than Ted.

The wine bottle opened with ease. She tended to get the corkscrew stuck more often than not and rip the cork itself to shreds, little tiny pieces falling into the bottle. She was surprised she got it out with one hard pull.

She filled two glasses and sighed with delightful happiness. Oh, this was a good white wine he picked. She glanced at the label. Expensive, too. The man had gone all out to apologize.

Well, like she told him outside, apology accepted. The flowers and doughnuts would've been enough of an apology. The wine, movie, and popcorn were an added bonus she wouldn't complain about.

The pizza finished cooking. The popcorn was popped. Her first glass of wine was consumed. Rory didn't come inside until her second glass was almost depleted.

She sighed in contentment when he wrapped his arms around her and kissed the side of her neck.

"Sorry, it took me so long. I talked with the officer who took the report. I waited for the tow truck to get here, then chatted with Reese for a bit about everything. Then the officer came back after knocking on a few houses. Nothing to report. We got nothing."

She twisted in his arms, almost sloshing some of the wine out of her glass. She giggled, then kissed him, rubbing her free hand across his scruffy face. It was slow and sweet and filled with all her hopes for what she wanted to happen —later, of course. They had to eat and everything.

"Is my beautiful Brooke on her way to being drunk

again?" he asked with a sexy grin that she wanted to imprint in her mind for eternity. She'd never get enough of this man's sweet, adorable grins. Sometimes cocky. Sometimes filled with heat. Sometimes even a touch of irritation and anger, yet like he was trying to hide it.

"I don't know why you think that."

His eyes grazed to the half-empty bottle, then cocked a brow.

"Well, okay, I'm on my second glass."

Because it had helped soothe her nerves while Rory dealt with the issue. Not something she wanted him to know, though. But the way his eyes drew down in concern, the way his grin turned into a slight frown, she knew he saw everything she wasn't saying.

"You owe me pizza and a movie," she said before he could comment on her frayed nerves, then stole a kiss.

"Cold pizza, it seems." Then he grabbed a slice behind her and took a bite. "You have magic hands, even with cold pizza."

"It was a cardboard pizza." She rolled her eyes. "Wait until I make you one with my own recipe for the dough."

"Can't wait." Then he narrowed his eyes at Willow who took that opportunity to jump back on the counter. "Get off the counter."

Meow.

Brooke chuckled. Rory growled.

"She never listens to me."

Brooke patted his scruffy cheek. "She never listens to me either. Don't take it personally."

He took another bite of pizza, then grabbed a plate she had set out on the counter. She took that as her cue they were going to start their romantic evening in.

They ventured to the living room with their plates of

pizza and a large bowl of popcorn. Rory had to make another trip with their glasses of wine. She slowed down on her intake of wine because she could. Rory was back by her side, and she already felt better. He made her feel safe and like everything was right in her world when everything was a bit off-kilter at the moment.

They watched the movie, cuddled together on the couch, and Brooke knew in that moment—if she hadn't already decided—she loved this man.

He could be arrogant and bossy, but also sweet and thoughtful.

Brooke couldn't ask for more.

13

"So, nothing, huh?" Reese asked as they headed inside the building.

Brooke had dropped him off at the auto shop where his vehicle had been towed last night. Jim, his mechanic, had replaced all four tires in time for him to grab it before work. He arrived at the same time as Reese to work.

"No, Officer Dorscher interviewed everyone home at the time and no one saw anything. There was no evidence to collect. The bastard. I'll get him for this."

Rory would not let Ted get away with this.

"While he keeps doing this shit to me and not Brooke, I can tell it freaks her out. She tries to hide it, but..." Rory shrugged. He saw it. No matter how hard she tried to hide her fears behind a sweet smile and cute laugh, he saw it.

"How'd 'operation forgive me' go last night?" Reese asked with a chuckle.

Rory wanted to smack that goofy-ass grin off his face. Reese knew it bugged him when he gave titles to everything. Mental box. Operation forgive me. Where did he come up with this shit?

"Great, actually. Although delayed, we did not let that stop us from having a good night. I'm thinking it's time to move this relationship up a bit."

Reese paused briefly before sitting down. "Move it up? Dude, you're already moving at light speed."

"Yeah, well, thanks to Ted, I want to move it even faster. It's shown me I like being around Brooke all the time, and I'm staying there every night anyway."

"So, like, you want to move in officially?"

"Yeah."

Reese shook his head and rolled his eyes.

"What?"

"You just met her. You dated Dawn for a year before you even proposed and look how that relationship turned out."

"There was a reason I waited so long. Maybe I knew it would never work out in the long run. Next time I'll follow my gut, which is what I'm doing. I'm going to stop at my place tonight and grab more stuff."

"Before you talk to Brooke?" Reese asked, his brow slowly rising.

"Yeah."

"Because she responds so well to your bossy ways."

Hmm. Reese had a point there. It would be better to have the conversation with her first, then grab some more things.

"Not to mention, you just bought that house."

That didn't matter to him at all.

"Her house is nicer and much homier. It has three bedrooms, enough space if we decide to have kids. My house only has two bedrooms. It shouldn't be hard to sell."

"Kids?"

Rory decided to ignore the surprise in Reese's voice.

"I love her, man. Like, love her. Yeah, it's fast. Yeah, it's crazy. But it's how I feel. Moving in, then marriage, and yeah, kids."

"As your best friend, I advise you to speak to her first before you do anything drastic, like put your house on the market."

Well, duh. Rory wasn't that dumb. But he had no worries. He knew things were moving very fast between him and Brooke, but it felt right. Although no words of love had been exchanged yet, he sensed Brooke felt the same way.

Willow, well, she was a different matter. If he wanted to win Brooke's heart completely, he'd have to win the dumb cat's heart as well.

She had a cat tower in the living room, but Rory thought Willow might enjoy one in the bedroom, too. They liked to hang out in the bedroom at night sometimes, watching a show or reading a book...or sex. Willow didn't like to be left out of anything. While he didn't like she was in the room when they got it on, he'd rather her curled up in a ball on a tower than sitting on the floor staring at them. She always seemed to relax and keep her eyes closed when she was sitting in her tower as if she were too comfortable to glare at him.

He had already ordered one this morning, set on the idea. He didn't think Brooke would complain—or Willow.

"Rory? Did you hear me?" Reese insisted as if he worried he'd do something dumb.

"Got it." Rory tapped his head. "Putting it in my mental box."

Reese rolled his eyes, yet laughed. "That's my line, not yours."

Rory tensed as Officer Brockman approached his desk with a morose expression.

"What's up?"

"I heard a call come through the radio. I recognized the address." His mouth turned grim. "It was yours. A neighbor called it in. Open door, broken front window."

"What the hell?"

Rory stood up, knocking his chair over. No words were spoken between him and Reese as they headed for his car. Reese didn't even bother arguing with him. There was no point because he wasn't going to let him drive.

When he arrived to his house, two patrol cars were in his driveway along with Susan's. Shit.

Officer Spencer nodded when he approached his front door. "It's not pretty."

He stepped inside and winced. Pictures on his walls were lying on the floor, glass littered everywhere. His couch was slashed from one end to the other. In his kitchen, the dishes were everywhere, smashed and broken, making it impossible to walk through without stepping on something. The food—what little food he had in the house since he hadn't been home in a while—was thrown about. The intense smell of sour milk had him leaving the area.

A trip upstairs showed him the same kind of treatment. His bed was slashed, foam everywhere. Feathers from his pillows dotted the floor. His clothes were strewn all over the floor, rips and tears over each item. The mirror in his bathroom was shattered. The water in the bathtub had been turned on and the plug in because there was water all over the floor. It had trailed to the hallway.

He went back downstairs where Susan was in the kitchen, dusting the back door for prints.

"Sorry, Rory. It's a mess. I know it looks like the water upstairs was running a long time, but I think your neighbors noticed it fairly quickly. Your front door was wide open and the window in the front is broken. It's pretty obvious from the sidewalk. Hopefully, not too much water damage," Susan said with an encouraging grin.

Shit. Rory didn't give a damn about the water damage or any of his other destroyed stuff. His fury was past his breaking point. He wanted to find Ted right this minute and destroy him. He didn't think Officer Dorscher even had time to find Ted's whereabouts yesterday when his tires were slashed. Because when he tried to question him last night, he hadn't been home. He had been planning this little adventure.

"Whatever you find, let me know ASAP," Rory snapped, hating himself for it, especially when Susan flinched and frowned. "I'm sorry. It's…" He let out a pained breath. "It's not your fault, and I'm sorry. You won't even find anything. Ted's been smart this whole time."

"If there's something to be found, I will."

Rory had no doubt about that. Susan was one of the best in the crime lab. He'd pick her over anyone else any day of the week.

He met Reese outside where he was talking with Officer Spencer.

"Anyone see anything?"

Reese shook his head. "Not your next door neighbor who called it in. Noticed your door wide open, walked up to it to see if you were home and saw the mess. Called the police right away. Zeke and Ben are on their way. They'll handle the case."

Rory nodded, knowing he couldn't since it was his house. The victim again.

"We know it was Ted."

"We keep assuming so," Reese replied.

"You don't think so?"

"It is the most obvious answer, especially since Officer

Dorscher couldn't locate him last night, and he just tried again after Spencer gave him a call. Ted still isn't home. But, you also tend to piss off a lot of people." Reese added a smile as if that would lessen the blow.

"I'm not that bad with people. I can be nice. I ain't no Mr. Fontain."

As soon as the words left his mouth, he and Reese shared a look.

"Brooke left work that night upset because he had touched her."

"Yeah, but she wasn't with Ted. How would he've found out?" Reese pointed out.

"He's obsessed with her, been following her around. I'm sure it wouldn't have been too hard for him to find out what happened. The entire office knew she left upset and they argued."

"Well, if he did find out somehow—because you're right, it would've been easy for him—he wouldn't have liked to know someone touched her like that. Just how he doesn't like it that you're dating her."

"But he hasn't physically come at Rory," Officer Spencer added.

"I'm also a cop. He knows it'll be harder to come at me. Not to mention, he didn't have to overpower Mr. Fontain. He was tied up because of Starla. It could've been a spur-of-the-moment kind of thing. Maybe he never intended to kill the guy, just rough him up or something. But, there he was, all tied up, easy enough for Ted to do what he needed to do."

"Then make it look like something it's not, putting that condom on him," Reese said.

"I want him found," Rory spit out at Spencer. A bit harsher than he intended, but it didn't appear to offend Spencer. He knew why Rory was pissed. Then Rory looked at Reese. "Let's relook at Mr. Fontain's case. Start tracking Ted's movement that day."

Because now that the idea was out in the open, Rory knew it fit.

Ted was so deranged, he killed a man because he had touched Brooke inappropriately.

What would Ted attempt to do next? He'd messed with his car—twice. And now his house.

He'd start watching his back because there was no telling what Ted might do next. And here he thought he had to worry about Brooke.

BROOKE SNUGGLED CLOSER, inhaling the succulent masculine scent she attributed to Rory only. A mixture of spice and cinnamon. She knew it came from his hair products because he used a few to make his hair smooth back so well all day. Even in the mornings before he got up to shower, she could still smell the lingering aroma from the day before.

She wasn't ready to get up yet. Even if the enticing smell would increase as he got ready for the day.

"I can feel your mind churning." He kissed the side of her head as his hand smoothed down her arm. "What's going on in that beautiful mind of yours?"

She inhaled again, although her nose wasn't close to his hair as her head was resting on his chest. She could still smell a hint of it.

"You smell good."

Rory chuckled. "Well, that's good." His laughter died. "That's it?"

She popped her head up. "I'm worried about you. I should bring you to and from work."

She knew that sounded silly the moment it slipped from her lips. He had a weapon and she barely could wield a fire poker. But still, she worried about him.

He cocked a brow, his expression telling her that was the most ridiculous thing he'd ever heard. "I'll be fine. Even though we didn't locate Ted yesterday, doesn't mean anything. He won't get the drop on me."

"He keyed your car, popped your tires, and broke into your home and trashed it. I would call that getting the drop on you."

"Insignificant stuff where he knew I wouldn't be around. He's nothing but a coward. Can't even try to come at me in person."

Brooke sat up some more, her brows dipping low. "That sounds like you want him to."

"I'm very eager to lock his ass up."

"Promise me you won't do something stupid."

"Hey." He sat up as well, brushing a hand across her cheek. "I'll be fine. I promise."

That was not what she asked him to promise. He could boss her around, follow her, and do things he thought were best for her, but when she asked—or tried to tell—him to do the same, he didn't listen.

"Do you think he killed Mr. Fontain because of me?" She couldn't picture it.

Well, to be fair, she couldn't picture Ted causing problems for Rory either, but obviously she didn't know Ted well at all. He had been a bit obsessive and controlling, which was why she broke up with him, so it made sense he would act out in the manner he was.

"I have no doubt in my mind he did. I have to prove it, though." Rory frowned. "We didn't get very far yesterday connecting him to it. He was at work, like usual, left on time at six o'clock. His neighbors said he came home around seven thirty, that they saw. No one reported seeing him leave throughout the night, but that doesn't mean he didn't. Mr. Fontain was killed late in the evening when most people were sleeping. Now that we can't locate him, it only adds to my suspicions."

Brooke would agree it was very odd Ted had disappeared. That proved he knew what he had done to Rory's house wouldn't go unpunished. The question remained, where did he run off to?

"How about I drive you to work?"

Her frown increased. "He's trying to hurt you, not me. I should be driving you to work."

"I can handle myself, sweetheart."

"Meaning I can't?" So like a man. She scooted out of bed before he could stop her.

"That's not what I said."

"Oh, you implied it by insisting you drive me to work, yet I can't drive you. It's not hard to read between the lines."

Then she headed for the bathroom and slammed the door. Because she could, and it made her feel better. For extra measure, she locked it. She couldn't deal with Rory and his arrogant attitude right now. He could protect her, but she couldn't protect him? Ugh. Men were idiots.

The doorknob shook.

"Brooke. Open the door."

The knob rattled again.

"Brooke. Now."

Oh, so bossy. Like she was going to listen to his demands, especially if he couldn't add a please to the end of it.

She undressed and turned on the shower.

"Brooke!" The knob shook. "Let's talk about this. Why are you mad at me?"

Before stepping into the shower, she stopped by the door but didn't unlock it. "I'm not mad. I need to get ready for work. You can use the bathroom down the hallway. I might be a while."

"This is ridiculous. Open the door...please."

Oh, now the man was getting smarter. She wasn't planning on unlocking the door, though. He didn't understand how she felt. That he could worry about her, but she couldn't do the same. If Ted had killed Mr. Fontain, then she had more than enough reason to worry about Rory.

When she hopped in the shower and continued to ignore him, he gave up. At least, she didn't hear the knob rattle any longer.

She screamed, dropping the shampoo bottle when a hand wrapped around her waist.

"It's just me," Rory whispered in her ear.

"How did you get in here?" The hot water hitting her didn't heat her up as much as his hard body snug behind hers did.

"I picked the lock. You can shut me out, but it doesn't mean it's going to keep me away. You're mad at me, and I don't like that."

A kiss hit her neck as his hands ventured to her breasts, kneading them, touching her nipples, igniting the burning desire she had before he had upset her to an inferno.

"I'm sorry." Another kiss hit her neck. "I know you can take care of yourself. Until we find Ted, I'll worry about you."

She twisted in his arms, enjoying the way the water hit her back and how he continued his raptured torture on her breasts.

"I worry about you, too."

"I know." He kissed her lips as if to stop himself from saying anything else. Smart man. He was working his way back into her good graces. She didn't want him to ruin it by saying something to upset her again.

Although, she should be mad at his audacity to pick the lock on the bathroom door. How could she have any privacy if she couldn't even be safe behind a locked door?

"Let me help you get clean." The delicious twinkle in his eyes as he grabbed the soap made her insides tingle with delight.

Oh, yes, he could help her all he wanted.

She had a feeling as he lathered up soap and started massaging her breasts, another kiss between them spiraling to new heights, that she'd be late to work today.

She didn't care for once.

"You're late," Reese commented as Rory took a seat at his desk.

He'd always be late if he had amazing sex in the shower with Brooke like he had this morning. He simply grinned at Reese, who understood his look immediately, rolling his eyes at the shit-eating grin.

"Any word on Ted?"

Not that he expected anything new because then he'd have to rip someone a new ass for not calling him first about it.

Reese shook his head.

Good. He didn't feel like hollering at anyone, not with the euphoric feeling still tingling in his veins.

"He probably skipped town."

Rory leaned back, contemplating that. "You think so? I'm dating the woman he's obsessed with. I don't think he's going to disappear and let me get away with that."

"Well, we looked hard yesterday for him. Checking with his friends, former coworkers, his family. Nobody has seen him, and any place they gave us as a potential hiding spot, he wasn't there."

"Doesn't mean he skipped town." Rory sat up and slammed the desk hard. "We don't even have shit on him either. Can't officially tie him to Mr. Fontain's murder, and gut instinct isn't going to cut it. Susan found a few prints in my house, but they could be mine. It'll take her some time to run everything. Besides that, she didn't find much other than all my shit is damaged."

"Well, he's dumb to go after a cop, but he has been a step ahead of us the entire time."

"He's deranged. I don't get it either. Nothing on his record suggests he would escalate to this level."

Reese shrugged. "Some people snap out of nowhere. Look at you. Fell hard for Brooke without even blinking. Obviously, so did Ted."

He did not like being compared with that asshole, but Reese had a point. There was something special about Brooke. Her adorable rambling, talking to her cat like it was her child. Her interesting intricacies about certain things, like taking out the garbage and touching raw meat. Her shyness, yet assertiveness when something ticked her off, like him bossing her around. Yeah, he fell hard for her. Because it was easy.

"Hey, guys. Got a sec," Doug said as he approached their desks.

"Got good news?" Reese asked, the eagerness plain in his tone.

Doug nodded. "We took your suggestion. Brought in Starla last night to talk to Dana. I don't know how she did it, but she got her to talk."

Rory liked hearing that. The only reason they knew Dana's name was because they ran her prints and found a missing person report on her from two years ago. She was so frightened, she wouldn't even tell them her name.

"That's great." Reese sat up straighter. "What'd you get from her?"

"Starla brought it on thick with her. Telling her about her sister and shit. Which I think is what helped. They've been threatening Dana's family, especially her sister if she ever tried to leave or talk. They scare them into obedience. Got a last-known location where they were housing Dana and some other women. Dana confirmed Starla's sister was one of the women there. They don't talk to each other, the assholes don't allow it, but she recognized Steph. We hit the place last night, but it was empty. They moved them, which didn't surprise us. It's been too long since we picked up Dana. It took too long to get her to tell us anything. She mentioned some other places they frequented, though. Different motels and such. There are too many places for us to get in one night, but there are two we want to watch tonight. You two up to help again? We don't plan to let any asshole get away this time."

"Count us in," Reese said before Rory could even say anything.

Not that he wouldn't help. This was important. Too many women's lives were at stake.

"Thanks, guys. I knew we could count on you. We're even pulling in Zeke, Ben, and Sauer to help. We need all the manpower we can get on this. They can't get away this time."

After giving them details—time and location—Doug left.

Reese looked happy. Rory wanted to express the same kind of excitement, yet he hesitated.

They abandoned their hideout in case Dana talked. Why wouldn't they do the same for the motels?

Maybe they'd get lucky tonight.

Rory hoped to get lucky all around and find Ted before tonight as well.

He wouldn't feel better until that asshole was off the street.

14

"YOU ALL DIDN'T HAVE to come over tonight," Brooke said as she sat down on the end of the couch, taking a sip of wine. She couldn't believe how much wine she'd had in the past few weeks since meeting Rory. But when it came to getting together with these ladies, it felt right.

Dee primped her hair and rolled her eyes. "It's what we do."

"What Dee means is, we all worry about our husbands, especially when it's something like this. It's easier to deal with when we're together," Rina said quietly, passing the bowl of popcorn toward Zoe, who couldn't quite reach it from her side of the couch.

Brooke might've gone overboard on snacks. Popcorn, chips, doughnuts, cookies, and even a dozen cupcakes sat all over her coffee table. There was barely room to set down their glasses. But hey, when she was stressed, she ate. A terrible habit, but she couldn't control it, no matter how hard she tried. And she loved food, so she figured it was futile to resist. Nobody had even questioned why she had all this junk food.

"They're all smart men. I'm sure everything will go smoothly tonight."

Brooke smiled at Mel. It was kind of her to say so, although she didn't have to worry like the rest of them. Newman wasn't a cop, so therefore he wasn't involved in the operation tonight. Yet, when Zoe and the other two knocked on her door, not more than an hour ago, she hadn't wanted to exclude Mel. She liked Mel and felt a connection with her the most. She brought a sense of comfort more than the other women. Susan was the only one not in attendance. She had to work.

"Zeke knows better than to not come home," Zoe said. "Plus, I promised I'd put on his favorite dress."

Rina and Dee giggled, leaving her and Mel frowning in confusion as if they were missing the joke, yet neither asked to clarify. Obviously a joke or something between those three—and Zeke.

"I'm sure it'll all go fine." Though Rina smiled, Brooke saw the worry in the lines stretched across her forehead and glittering in her eyes.

"I'm sure you're right." Then Brooke grabbed a doughnut and stuffed it into her mouth before she voiced the concern worming its way inside.

"Oh, hello, beautiful," Mel cooed as Willow came by her where she sat on the floor.

Brooke had offered her spot, but Mel insisted she was fine on the floor. Brooke sat next to Rina, who sat next to Dee. Zoe sat on her recliner next to the couch. It made Brooke realize she'd have to get a larger couch if this was going to be a reoccurrence in the future. Nobody should have to sit on the floor. She had even offered to grab a chair from the kitchen, but Mel shook that suggestion off as well.

"So, what's up with the douchecanoe?" Dee asked out of nowhere, looking at Brooke.

Brooke's brows rose, her eyes widening.

Wow. She didn't have high opinions about Rory.

Then Dee chuckled. "I'm talking about Ted."

Brooke still looked taken aback. What about him? Was she talking about the restraining order?

"Dee has no filter if you've noticed," Zoe said with a chuckle, eyeing Dee with a look that said she should settle down. But then Zoe turned back toward her. "So, any news? Don't look so surprised, Brooke. The guys are just as bad about gossip as we are. Plus, they worry more than they'll ever admit to us. Something happens to one of us, everyone finds out. We know about Ted and that Rory thinks he killed your boss."

Apparently, they were switching conversations. Not one she wanted to have. But by the engaging looks she was getting from each woman, she wasn't going to be able to escape it.

"I don't think they've found him yet. Rory and Reese were asking questions around the office again yesterday. People were still buzzing about it today. I mean, about Mr. Fontain, not Ted. Nobody at my office had met Ted. Mr. Fontain hadn't even met Ted, so I'm not even sure how Ted knew where to find him. Like, how did he know where he lived? And why hurt him? It's not like I told Ted what Mr. Fontain had done to me."

"Cockroaches always find a way," Dee said, then ruffled her hair a bit. "And if he's as crazy obsessive as he sounds, then he was following you."

"Dee," Rina said in a very soft, yet berating voice as if telling Dee to stop.

Dee shrugged. "What, it's true." Then she looked

chagrined and smiled at Brooke. "I'm sorry if that was too blunt."

Brooke shrugged. "Blunt but honest. He probably was." Then a shiver rippled through her. "Which is why I worry about Rory. If Ted did kill Mr. Fontain, he could hurt Rory, too."

Dee waved her hand frivolously in the air. "Rory's too stubborn to get hurt like that. He's worse than Zeke."

"Hey," Zoe admonished, slapping Dee on the knee.

Dee shrugged and laughed, yet didn't take back her words.

Willow jumped up on the coffee table, finding an empty spot to do so, surprisingly.

"Naughty kitty," Brooke said as she shooed her hand at Willow. "Get down."

Willow meowed as she jumped off, then sauntered out of the living room as if she wasn't hollered at and had better things to do with her time than hang with them.

"I like your hair, Brooke," Rina said.

Oh, she was happy for the conversation change now.

She shuffled a hand through her hair as a shy smile appeared. "Mel and I had a fun night a few days ago."

"Super fun," Mel giggled.

"It does look good on you. Doing something like that would clash with my red hair." Dee sighed, primping her hair once again.

"You could try green during Christmas," Zoe said. Although she couldn't say it with a straight face.

Dee glared at her.

She, Mel, and Rina couldn't hold back a small laugh.

A loud knock on her door had them all falling silent. Brooke took a sip of wine instead of standing up. She even wanted to reach for a doughnut.

"Are you going to get the door?" Rina asked, a bit of trepidation in her soft tone.

"Shit, are you even expecting anyone?" Dee asked sharply, looking ready to jump up and defend her against the potential evil behind the door.

Such a contrast to Rina's soft-spoken words.

Brooke shook her head, then stood up. Her mind had immediately flashed to Ted, being brazen enough to show up after all the chaos he had caused for Rory. But why should she be afraid? She was surrounded by her friends. Plus, she had her poker.

"Want me to get it?" Dee asked, perched on the edge of her seat, yet waiting, as if not wanting to overstep her boundary.

"I'll get it." Brooke set her glass between a bag of potato chips and the doughnuts. Then grabbed the fire poker.

"Girl, I like how you think," Dee said with a chuckle.

"You can never be too safe."

Then she headed for the front door, her heart pounding, her hands suddenly sweaty. Hopefully, the dumb poker didn't slip right through her fingers.

THIS TIME some officers sat in a room on the first level of the motel, so when the car pulled into the lot and dropped off a woman, they'd be able to nab the driver before he could pull out of the lot. That's *if* they showed up tonight. They hadn't had much time to start surveillance on either location, but they didn't want to waste any time this time. So, the more help they had on this, the better.

Rory and Reese sat across the street once again and

would move in on the location as soon as Doug gave the all-clear.

The van they sat in with Doug and Todd was quiet this time around. Nobody spoke, not even him and Reese. There wasn't a lot to say. They wanted these bastards caught—today—before the women had to endure any more pain and suffering. Using the term women was very loose as well, as some of them pulled off the streets were still little girls. The bastards dressed them up to look older than they were. Some men liked underage girls. Sick, sick bastards.

The night dragged on at both locations. Nothing out of the ordinary occurred. People walking along the street, cars passing by in a blur. The motel lights shining, the 'vacancy' sign lit up, yet no customers appearing.

Rory did his best watching the monitors, helping to look for a sign of anything strange. Yet, his mind kept wandering to Brooke and how she was holding up. He had gotten a text from Zeke telling him Zoe and the other ladies had shown up at Brooke's house. She was safe and most likely having fun. That had helped settle his worries some, but not all of them. Ted was still out there. As long as Ted was wandering about, planning and causing havoc, the tension and fear would remain inside his soul.

The last thing he needed to be doing was pushing Brooke away—without even meaning to. He appreciated her worry, but it wasn't necessary. He could take care of himself. To think she thought she had to drive him to work was so laughable, yet he was a smarter man than that. He would never laugh about something like that to her face, but if this morning was any clue, he'd do well to mind his words as well. Because she hadn't liked his blasé attitude about it.

He didn't want to argue with her about something like who was driving and who wasn't.

Locking him out of the bathroom—shutting him out like that—oh, hell, no. He never wanted her to do that again. It had bruised his heart. Reminding him he had to tread carefully with her. Just because she appeared meek and mild about some things didn't mean she was. When push came to shove, she would show her claws—like Willow.

"Car's pulling in. Everyone stand by," Doug said sharply, leaning toward the monitors in front of them, his gaze intense.

It was impossible to see who was behind the wheel. The darkness didn't help, plus it appeared the car had tinted windows. A good sign they might have hit their mark finally. The car sat idle for a few minutes, making the tension in the van palpable. *Make a move already*. Rory was sure everyone wanted to shout it.

After what felt like ages, a woman got out and walked toward the stairs leading to the second level. They hadn't seen anyone else arrive, so her paying client wasn't here yet. And she definitely looked like what they were waiting for. Tight, short dress. High heels. Her steps weren't as steady as they could be. Either she wasn't used to heels yet, or she was high, which Rory wouldn't doubt. Dana had been under the influence of some heavy narcotics when they rescued her. It was one of the many ways they kept the women under their thumb. Keeping them drugged helped to control them better.

She knocked on the door and it opened a few seconds later.

Everyone perked up at that.

"We didn't see anyone arrive before her," Todd nearly shouted.

Which meant whoever was in the room with her had

been waiting a while for her to get here, having arrived before they had.

The car started to move.

"Now!" Doug shouted into the radio.

The three cops waiting in one of the rooms ran out, guns drawn, stepping into the car's path before it could gain momentum.

Rory and the rest of them in the van didn't wait either. They all rushed out of the van and across the street. There were more cops behind the motel as well, waiting. They all rained down on the tiny motel.

Out of nowhere, shots rang out. They had made it to the parking lot, barely taking cover behind a parked car. Except the shots had come from behind them, not from the motel.

Of course, the guy behind the wheel hadn't listened to step out of the vehicle. He took that opportunity to pull his weapon as well and started firing.

All hell broke loose.

Rory was pinned down with Reese behind a car as shots from across the street kept coming.

"Shit. They had their own lookout man," Reese muttered, as he ventured a small look around the car, jumping back when more shots dinged the car.

"Do we know where the shots are coming from?" He fell flat to the ground, trying to peer from underneath the car, but couldn't see much. Maybe if he crawled farther under... No, he didn't feel like taking a bullet to the head tonight.

"Anyone got a good look at the shooter across the street?" Reese asked into his radio.

The guy in the car had stopped firing, as had the cops who had surrounded the vehicle. The bullets shattered in the windshield said the guy didn't make it.

Which sucked.

Now they had to get the shooter across the street alive or they'd be back at square one trying to nab these bastards.

"We're crossing the street now. It looks like someone sitting in a black sedan, the window halfway down, but can't get a good look at his face. Shit!" Someone crackled into the radio.

By the squealing of tires that rented the air, Rory could only assume the car was driving away.

Shit was right.

But his colleagues were on top of their game. The license plate number rattled through the radio, sending out an alert to every cop to keep a lookout. A few seconds later, the owner of the vehicle—as someone had immediately run the plates—came through the radio.

Ted.

"What the hell was he doing here?" Rory spat, then stood up, his knees starting to hurt from crouching so long.

Reese looked at him with a frown, then pointed toward his sleeve. "I would guess to kill you if the blood on your arm is a clue. Shit, Rory. You were shot."

Rory glanced at his arm, eyeing the blood seeping through a tear in his jacket and the bit of white from his shirt. It didn't hurt too much, which is why he didn't even notice. But now that he could see it, a sharp pain hit his system. Like a nasty rug burn. The adrenaline from trying not to get shot must've hidden the pain. Now that the threat was gone and the tension wasn't as high, everything was coming back into focus.

He moved his arm a bit, the ache increasing.

"It's just a graze."

A very annoying, painful graze.

"Well, if we weren't a hundred percent sure he killed Mr. Fontain, I'd say we are now."

And he got away.

That man was going down—tonight!

15

BROOKE LET OUT her breath in slow increments as she came face to face with Adam, Mel's brother, and his friend whose name she couldn't quite remember.

"Oh, hi. Hi. Hello." Brooke laughed, feeling like a big idiot. One, for bringing a poker to the door, which Adam had glanced at. Two, for saying hi too many times.

"Uh, hi." Adam cleared his throat, eyeing the poker again. "Is Mel here?"

"Yeah, she is. Come on in. Don't mind this," she said with another lame laugh. "I was going to stoke the fire...that I haven't started yet."

"It's the end of May." The way Adam quirked his brows in confusion had Brooke feeling even stupider.

She should stop talking.

"Mel! It's Adam."

Then she walked away, hoping to find some dignity left.

"What's up? You okay?" Mel asked Adam, standing up from the floor.

He gave an odd smile to all the women, then nodded at Mel. "Nick and I wanted to head to the skate park down the road but wanted to grab some drinks first at the gas station. I don't have any money on me."

He looked at his feet as if he hated asking for some.

"Dishes for two weeks and I'll give you a twenty," Mel replied, grabbing her purse that sat on the floor near the coffee table.

He rolled his eyes. "One week."

"Oh, ten it is, then." Mel started to dig for her wallet.

"Fine," he mumbled. "Dishes one week, garbage the other. For twenty."

Mel smiled. "Garbage isn't as hard as dishes. Dishes one week, garbage *and* mow the lawn one week, and you have a deal."

"That doesn't seem fair," he grumbled.

"Shit, I agree. Mowing the lawn is harder than all that," Dee piped in as if she had a right.

Brooke chuckled, then coughed, trying to hide she did so.

Mel gave Dee the stink eye, then back to Adam, producing a grin that said she wasn't going to budge. Good for her, Brooke thought. Raising a teenager couldn't be easy, especially when said teenager was her brother and had gone through some traumatic stuff. Deadbeat dad. Mom in prison. Getting kidnapped because the kids in the town didn't like him. Rough life. Brooke had nothing to complain about when she looked at Adam's story.

"Fine, okay. Dishes for two weeks." He held out his hand, rolling his eyes again.

Mel enhanced her smile and gave him a twenty. "Don't stay out too late. Don't talk to anyone you don't know. Call me if you have any problems. Maybe I should pick you up from the park later."

"We're cool, Mel. Chill." Then he headed for the door. "Thanks, sis. Don't *you* stay out too late."

The door shut and the boys were gone.

"That boy has such an attitude sometimes." Yet Mel didn't say it like it was a bad thing. The smile on her face said she was still mooning over winning the fight with him. Her original deal, too, with doing the dishes for two weeks.

Brooke hated doing the dishes. She wished she had someone to do hers for two weeks. She'd pay twenty bucks for that. Maybe she could get Adam to do hers, too. Or his friend, Nick, who happened to live a block over from her.

"I'll pay him to mow my lawn for twenty," Dee said with a snicker.

"He needs to learn the value of money and hard work. Nothing comes easy in life." Mel's smile dimmed. "I know he knows that. But I don't want to hand him things and make everything easy because he's had it hard. I can't make him think I'm feeling sorry for him or something. He'll thank me later when he's older. And if you want to pay him twenty a week to mow your lawn, have at it. It's not my money."

"I might. I'll mention it to Sauer."

"He can't drive," Mel reminded her. "So you'll have to pick him up and stuff."

"I think—"

Zoe's phone ringing cut off whatever Dee was going to reply. She answered it, her facial expression going from happiness to shock said it was Zeke, but he wasn't relaying good news.

She hung up and looked at Brooke.

"What?" Brooke didn't like the look on her face.

"Rory was shot."

The air stilled. Or maybe it was her breath. Silence descended.

Then a scream rented the air—her scream.

A nasty, aching pain shot through her body.

"Brooke!"

She thought it was Mel who screamed her name, but she couldn't be sure as she stared at her foot where the poker fell from her hand and landed on her foot.

The room shifted and then nothing but blackness.

"Only two stitches. Not enough to claim as a war wound."

Rory rolled his eyes at Reese as he sat on the edge of the hospital bed. His arm felt stiff and achy. The bullet only grazed him, thankfully. A big enough graze that required a trip to the hospital and two stitches. The doctor prescribed some pain medication and Rory had already taken some the nurse had given him. He didn't care if anyone called him a baby. Getting shot—even a graze—hurt like a bitch.

Although he hadn't wanted to come to the hospital, Reese made him. But that wouldn't stop him from leaving and heading to the crime scene. He had missed all the good stuff, and quite frankly, it pissed him off.

"Hey, how's the arm?" Zeke said with an easy grin as he popped his head into the room.

"I'll survive." Rory stood up and grabbed his jacket but didn't put it on. It hurt too much to move his arm—even something simple like slipping his arm through a sleeve— and he'd rather not display any pain in front of his friends.

"So..." Zeke started, yet didn't finish as his brows drew low along with his gaze.

"So..." Rory mimicked, cocking a brow.

What was up with Zeke? Reese was also staring at Zeke curiously.

"I might've called Zoe after everything went down at the motel. She might've relayed some of it to Brooke."

Great. Just what he needed. Brooke finding out a bullet grazed him. She'd never want him to participate in another raid ever again. Oddly enough, the sharp pain that pierced his heart at the thought of her fear had him thinking he wouldn't do such a thing again—not if it upset her.

"How upset is she?" Rory had to be as prepared as possible, finding the right words to use before he saw her.

"Well," Zeke winced, "she's here. In the hospital."

"Shit." Rory ran a tired hand down his face with his good arm. That wasn't enough time to come up with a good explanation that would downplay how intense it had been.

"Umm...I don't think you understand me, Rory."

Rory dropped his hand and looked at Zeke. "Excuse me?"

Zeke cleared his throat, shifting on his feet. He was nervous. Rory could count on one hand how many times he had seen Zeke Chance nervous.

"So, Zoe said you got shot, but didn't have enough time to tell Brooke it was only a graze. It kind of freaked Brooke out and she dropped the poker she was holding onto her foot. So, she's not here to see you, per se. She's here getting her foot looked at." Zeke added a smile as if that would make the words he spoke sound better than they were.

Rory's hands fisted, sending shooting pain through his injured arm, yet he couldn't stop the motion, no matter how hard he tried. Keeping his cool took more of his strength at the moment.

"Let me get this straight. Your wife told Brooke I got shot. She then hurt herself with a poker she was holding. Why was she holding the damn poker?"

That was more of a rhetorical question. Because of Ted.

Well, she didn't have that to worry about anymore.

"Where is she?" he snapped, then forced himself to unclench his fists because the pain slicing through his arm was finally getting to be too much.

"Down the hall and to the right. Second door on the left."

Rory stalked past Zeke and heard footsteps behind him. He figured it to be Reese. He hoped Zeke was smart enough to know he didn't want him following him. Not when he was the cause of this mishap by telling his wife he got shot.

When he walked into the room, he saw Mel on one side of the bed and Rina on the other.

"Brooke." Her name came out more in a whisper than he anticipated. It's as if all his energy had been zapped walking from his room to hers.

She looked up. Surprise, relief, and what he swore was love shining in her beautiful emerald depths bore into him.

Mel and Rina exited the room without a word.

Although it pained him—greatly—both of his arms went around her, holding her tight. A muffled cry slipped from her lips, and as much as he didn't want her to cry, he knew what she was feeling. He wanted to cry a little himself. She could've severely hurt herself. Actually, he didn't know how badly she had hurt herself. He was too afraid to pull away and ask. Not to mention, he could've hurt himself much worse as well. The graze could've been a full dead-on shot. Pierced his chest instead of his arm. Anything could've happened.

He could've lost her tonight and without telling her how he felt.

He pulled away and grasped her cheeks, wincing as he did, yet it didn't stop him. He didn't lower his injured arm, no matter how much the pain sliced up and down like a raging flow of hot lava burning his skin.

"I love you. I love you so damn much." His lips touched hers softly, like the brush of a flower petal against one's skin. "Tell me you love me too."

Her smile against his lips made his heart skip a beat, anticipating hearing the words. "That sounded like a demand to do so."

He moved away enough to see her eyes. "A request, not a demand."

She grabbed both of his hands and made him lower them to her lap. Tenderness touched her gaze as he winced by the movement, but it felt much better to have his arm to his side.

"You gave me quite a scare today. Or Zoe did when she said what she said. Then I dropped the poker on my foot. It hurt, and I fainted. That hurt because no one was around to catch my fall. My head hurts. My foot hurts. It's not broken, if you're wondering. I bruised it. Thank goodness the poker wasn't sharper or it would've gone right through my foot. I feel so stupid, dropping it in front of everyone. I'm sure they—"

He brushed his lips across hers once again. Not hard and bruising as his heart felt at the moment not hearing the words he wanted to hear, but soft and delicate knowing he needed to tread lightly with her. She only rambled when she was nervous.

Why was she nervous? It could only mean one thing.

She didn't love him. Which was why she hadn't said it yet.

"I know I can be bossy and sometimes arrogant. I probably won't change." He offered a grin to lighten the blow, but hey, he knew himself. He was who he was and wouldn't apologize for it. "But I love you. I will love you until my dying day. That I know. I will protect you and care for you, and even love that crazy, psychotic cat of yours." His grin inched up a notch at the way her brow rose, her eyes narrowing. "I hope you love me the same. Tell me you love me the same."

That time his words did sound a bit more demanding, urging her to say it.

He needed her to say it. Because he wouldn't be able to walk away from her. While he wouldn't go as far or as obsessive as Ted, he'd go crazy without Brooke in his life.

"Don't ever get shot again." Her expression was very stern.

"Grazed, but I won't." Although he didn't add the word promise because he couldn't promise something like that. Anything could happen.

His heart pounded. His mind conquered too many scenarios of what he'd do if she told him she didn't love him. Maybe he would go as crazy as Ted.

"I love you, too, Rory." Then she bent her head until it rested on his chest, sighing as if content. "Your heart's racing."

"Afraid you didn't love me."

Her arms wrapped around him, as she pressed closer. "I swear my heart's been racing since Zoe told me you were hurt. I don't like this feeling, Rory."

Yeah, he could agree. He didn't like knowing she got hurt either.

"I'm okay. Everything turned out fine."

He groaned, almost a whine when she sat up. He liked holding her like that. It reaffirmed everything she said—that she loved him. He could feel it in her tight embrace, clinging to him as though if she didn't, he might mysteriously disappear.

"What happened?"

His lips turned down, his brows drawing low as he thought of everything that happened today. It was a lot, especially for a conversation in a small ER room.

"The raid was going down fine until bullets started flying." He sighed. "Ted showed up and created chaos. I got grazed in it all. The trafficker we were trying to arrest was killed, and Ted got away."

She shook her head, her eyes wide. "I can't believe him. Why won't he stop?"

Rory grabbed one of her hands and pulled it to his lips, using his good arm. Although, he would've endured the pain to touch her anywhere with his lips.

"He can't hurt anyone ever again."

She frowned. "You said he got away."

"He did. But we—well, not me, damn it—caught up to him. They gave chase and he ended up crashing his car. He didn't survive the crash, I'm told. I was planning to head to the scene as soon as they discharged me."

A shiver wracked her body, making him tighten his grip on her hand. "When were you planning on calling me? Telling me all of this?"

He produced a sexy grin, the ones he loved to pull out when he knew he was going to be in trouble. "I would never keep you in the dark, sweetheart."

"Mm-hmm. Sure you wouldn't."

His grin widened. "I love you."

"Saying those three little words—that I love hearing—is not going to get you out of the cathouse every single time."

Cathouse? He chuckled. Only his Brooke—lover of cats

—would say cathouse instead of doghouse. He pressed his lips to hers. "But it will this time, right?"

"Perhaps," she murmured against his mouth.

He squeezed her hand. "No more touting that poker around. You don't need it. Plus, it's not safe." This time he produced a lopsided grin. "Can't trust you with a knife or a poker. I cut the meat. I start all fires and maintain them from now on. Got it."

"As long as that was a request and not a demand," she replied with a sultry grin.

"Of course."

She cocked a brow at his response, but he didn't clarify which one he meant. Because no matter how hard he tried, he'd have a hard time asking nicely, especially when it came to her safety.

She pursed her lips in a comical manner as if she wanted to hold back laughter, yet her brow was still cocked, maintaining a stern expression.

Oh, how he loved this woman.

Sweet and funny. Obstinate and firm. Non-stop chatter to tongue-tied. She was so many things, and he couldn't wait to unravel more delightful traits she possessed for the next fifty years and beyond.

"Let's go home. We both need to heal. I got shot, and you got stabbed."

She rolled her eyes at his over-exaggeration of injuries, but it wasn't far off the truth. Both things could've happened.

Life was precious and sometimes all too short. He planned to live his to the fullest with Brooke by his side.

EPILOGUE

Two weeks later

"EVERYTHING IS GOING to be fine. It all looks perfect. Come here." Rory was finally able to grab a hold of Brooke's arm as she bustled to and from the kitchen to the living room.

He wrapped his arms around her, pressed his lips to her neck, and inhaled the sweet succulent scent of roses. He knew why she smelled like roses. Because, besides the new cat tower he bought Willow for the bedroom, he had also purchased Brooke a deluxe home spa treatment. While she hadn't broken her foot, it had been heavily bruised. The doctor had told her to be gentle on it for at least a week. He thought soaking in the tub would help. Plus, she enjoyed her baths. Her foot was feeling better, but she had taken a relaxing bath this afternoon with one of the rose bath bombs.

Now all he wanted to do was keep inhaling her beautiful scent, wrap her up in his arms, and take her upstairs to make sweet, sweet love with her.

Except he couldn't.

Everyone would be coming over soon for game night. Zeke and everyone liked to rotate who hosted, and today was his and Brooke's turn. It was nice to get together once a week with friends. Although this was only their second time getting together for game night, Rory decided he liked it. Because it put a smile on Brooke's face. Her excitement and glee when he offered to have it at their house this time couldn't be forgotten. It had filled his heart with so much love and joy he couldn't believe he had lived without the wonderful feeling as long as he had. That he never realized love could be so beautiful and magical as it was with Brooke. It had been nowhere near this level with Dawn.

His lips started to trail up her neck, across her cheek, to her lips when she pushed on his chest. A mixture of a groan and growl escaped as he turned his lips into a pout.

"No distracting me. You'll get some later, I have no doubt. I need to put this in the oven." Then she twisted out of his arms and shoved a cookie sheet full of mozzarella sticks into the oven. "Can you make sure I set out the veggie tray in the dining room?"

"Check. Already saw it."

She stood up, her brow arched in the most delectable way, with a hand on her hip. "Double check."

"Was that a request or a demand?"

"Now." Then she turned around and went about another task that had her reaching into the fridge.

Deciding it was better not to tempt the beast—it had been a demand—he walked out of the kitchen and saw the veggie tray was sitting in the same spot as the last time he saw it.

"It's here."

Meow.

He glanced down at Willow who sat near the table.

"Nope. You can't have any more treats. And if I see you attempt to jump up on that table, I won't sneak you any more either. Got it?"

Meow.

Then Willow stood up and sauntered off with her tail high in the air.

"You're lucky I love your mother."

"What's that?" Brooke asked as she whizzed by him, setting a tray of cheese and crackers next to the veggie tray.

"Nothing. Just observing how wonderful everything looks. Why don't you take a break?"

"I need to check on the mozzarella sticks."

Before he could tell her she just put them in the oven, she walked away *and* the doorbell went off.

"Get that. Thanks. Love you. You're the best."

Well, he was going to answer the door regardless, but he always loved hearing she loved him—and he never minded hearing he was the best either.

Reese stood on the porch with a six-pack of craft beer he loved and a cheesy-ass grin. "Game night. I feel so honored to be invited." Then his smile dipped a fraction. "Although I will be the only one without a significant other. Not sure what I think about that."

"Well, I'd feel pathetic. Thanks for coming, buddy." He clapped Reese on the back as he ushered him inside, laughing at the annoyance on his face.

"You're a terrible friend. I'm putting this moment in my mental box for later."

"You and that damn box." He gestured at the beer. "Want me to put that in the fridge?"

Reese half shrugged and handed it over. Rory headed to a small mini-fridge Brooke had purchased for the party. When she had a party, she went all out. He figured most of it was nerves and wanting everything to go off without a hitch. She didn't have many friends and now she did. She wanted everything perfect. To a T.

"You could've asked Starla to come."

Reese looked at him like a deer in headlights, then looked away. "No, I don't think so."

By the touch of sadness in his tone, Rory decided not to press the issue. He had an inkling—getting bigger as time went on—that Reese liked Starla. The last raid they thought had ended badly because the guy in the car had been killed had turned out amazing as if they had received an A+ on a really hard test. The woman, unlike the previous one, had spoken up right away. Told them her last known location where they apprehended six men who were holding fifteen women in a small rundown house on the outskirts of town. One of the women had been Starla's sister, Steph. Reese had been in contact with Starla the one time to tell her they found her sister, and after that, nothing. Yet, Rory knew when his best friend liked a woman, and he'd bet every last dollar he had—and his relationship with Brooke—that his friend liked Starla.

Rory handed him one of the beers he had brought. "Make sure you tell Brooke everything looks amazing or I'll kick your ass."

Reese chuckled and nodded. Either in thanks for the beer or in agreement he would. Rory took it as both.

"Everything does look amazing. Look at all the food. I'm glad I didn't eat before I came."

"Yeah," Rory said with laughter. "She went overboard with the food. But I think she's nervous and wants everything to go well. Which it will."

"Because you say so."

"Damn right."

They laughed together.

"So, Susan called you earlier, right?"

Rory nodded, unable to hide his shit-eating grin. "Oh, yeah. Woke me up with the news, which I didn't mind at all."

Sometimes processing evidence moved slowly. After getting Ted's DNA sample when he crashed and died, Susan was able to cross-reference that with the DNA found on the tie wrapped around Mr. Fontain's neck. A perfect match. Which proved Ted had been there and killed the man. They still weren't sure how he knew Mr. Fontain touched Brooke inappropriately, but it didn't matter in the end. They knew he killed him and could close the case.

Brook came into the room and shrieked. "You're here. Reese is here, Rory."

"I know." Then he smiled when she looked at him like he had done something wrong. "I love you."

She started to giggle, yet her eyes started to water like she was on the verge of tears. He stalked to her in three long steps, grabbing her hands.

"Everything is going to be perfect. It already is."

"I'm acting silly, aren't I?" she whispered, not wanting Reese to hear.

"You're beautiful and doing a wonderful job."

His lips barely brushed hers because she was suddenly zooming by him to answer the doorbell. He could only chuckle and shrug when he shared a look with Reese. Soon enough, everyone had arrived. The guys had decided to take a seat in the living room enjoying the chips and dip, popcorn, and large pretzels situated in the room. The women gathered around the dining room table.

As both rooms were semi-connected together, Brooke clapped her hands to get everyone's attention. "Before we get to the big game, charades, I thought another game in between would be fun. You can't say the words 'taste' or 'case.' I'm going to pass out a chip clip to everyone." Brooke shrugged, her cheeks tinting red. "It's all I have, and I have a lot." Then she laughed. "If you say the word, you have to give your chip clip to the other person who caught you. I have a special prize for the winner at the end."

"Can we keep the chip clips?" Ben asked. "Because I swear I'm always losing ours."

A few people laughed with him, as if they misplaced theirs as well.

"Maybe a few," Brooke said with a sweet smile.

Rory decided he wouldn't let anyone leave with more than one. They could buy their own. And no one would be taking the cute black cat chip clips he had purchased last week when he saw them hanging in the grocery store chip aisle. It immediately reminded him of Brooke and Willow, and yeah. He'd fight to the death if someone tried to take those as their winnings.

"Let's get this party started. I know I won't say either word because I plan to win," Dee shouted, her facial expression mired in determination. She was in it to win it.

Rory had a feeling he might fail. Last time, the guys had talked about different cases a lot, something he had mentioned to Brooke. Probably one of the reasons she picked the word 'case.' And 'taste,' that one was pretty easy to figure out as well. A lot of great food was scattered around the house. It would be impossible not to say how amazing everything tasted.

When he saw the beaming smile on Brooke's face, he wanted to walk across the room, pull her into his arms, and kiss her senseless. Tell her how much he loved her and how blessed he was to have found her before it was too late.

Of course, he didn't want to make a scene.

Then he heard Zeke mention how awesome the homemade chili cheese dip tasted, and Rory decided he was in it to win it as well.

"You said the word," he pointed out, snapping his fingers at Zeke's chip clip.

He caught Brooke's sweet smile, her eyes giddy with happiness, and thought, screw it. He snatched the chip clip out of Zeke's hand and stalked to Brooke in four long strides, pulling her into his embrace.

"I love you." Then he sealed the words with a delicious kiss that had him wanting more. So much more that he couldn't do in a room full of people.

***

LOOKING for another exciting romantic suspense series? I have the perfect one for you. A small town romance series with edge of your seat suspense!

WELCOME TO LUCKY...WHERE DANGER LURKS IN THE SHADOWS. START WITH ESCAPING MEMORIES TODAY!

FOR ZEKE AND ZOE'S STORY
WON'T LET YOU GO
A SLAYING LOVE NOVEL, #1

A determined detective. A woman refusing to bend. A killer who will make sure there are no second chances.

One night of passion became Zoe Sullivan's worst nightmare when Detective Zeke Chance mistook her for a prostitute. Now she wants nothing more than to forget the humiliation —and the man who caused it. But when her boss is brutally murdered, fate throws them together again as Zeke becomes the lead detective on the case.

Zeke knows he screwed up royally, and he's determined to make amends while keeping Zoe safe. But as the investigation deepens, it becomes clear that someone wants Zoe silenced permanently. With a killer closing in and their undeniable attraction reigniting, Zeke must overcome Zoe's distrust before they both become the next victims.

As danger escalates and passion burns hotter than ever, they'll discover that some mistakes are worth making twice —if they survive long enough to get their second chance.

Get ready for steamy romance, heart-pounding suspense, and a detective who'll risk everything to earn back the woman he wronged.

FOR BEN & RINA'S STORY
DOOMED LOVE
A SLAYING LOVE NOVEL, #2

A protective detective. A woman with dangerous secrets. A killer who will stop at nothing to have his way.

Detective Ben Stoyer has wanted Rina Chastain for far too long, but she keeps turning him down with sweet excuses he's tired of hearing. When the victim in his latest murder case looks exactly like her, Ben's protective instincts kick into overdrive—and this time, he won't take no for an answer.

Rina wants to give in to Ben's relentless charm, but her controlling father has destroyed every relationship she's ever tried to have. Now, with a serial killer targeting women who look like her, she's caught between the detective who's determined to protect her and the man who's determined to control her.

As the body count rises and Ben's investigation intensifies, they'll discover that some dangers come from within, and the deadliest enemy might be the one you trust most.

Get ready for pulse-pounding suspense, sizzling chemistry, and a detective who'll defy everyone—including the woman he loves—to keep her safe.

FOR SAUER & DEE'S STORY
DEADLY CRAZY
A SLAYING LOVE NOVEL, #3

A sassy woman who doesn't believe in love. A shy detective who'll die to protect her. A killer who picked the wrong target.

Dee O'Malley has learned the hard way that men don't stick around, so she's not about to risk her heart on sweet, shy Detective Sauer—even if his kisses make her believe in impossible things. When she's brutally attacked, Dee's determined to find the bastard herself, even if it drives her would-be protector crazy. After all, he's adorable when he's worried.

Detective Sauer might be tongue-tied around most women, but loud, fearless Dee O'Malley turns him into a stammering mess for all the right reasons. The moment she's hurt, his shyness vanishes and his protective instincts take over. But when the attack connects to one of his murder cases, Sauer realizes keeping Dee safe means keeping her close—and his biggest obstacle might be Dee herself.

As the threat escalates and Dee refuses to back down, they'll learn that sometimes the most dangerous thing you can do is fall in love with someone who's willing to die for you.

Get ready for sharp-tongued banter, explosive chemistry, and a shy detective who transforms into a fierce protector when the woman he loves is threatened.

For Stitch & Susan's Story

EVIDENCE OF SIN

A SLAYING LOVE NOVEL, #4

A tattooed bad boy with a record. A police department analyst who should know better. A killer who's making it personal.

One night of scorching passion with straight-laced Susan left tattoo artist Stitch running scared—straight out of her life. But now he's back, and everything about the woman he can't forget terrifies him in the best possible way. She's law enforcement, he's got a record—they'll never work, but when she's in his arms, none of it matters.

Susan knew getting involved with Stitch wouldn't end well, but she can't resist the way he makes her feel alive with just one heated look. She should be focusing on the latest string of brutal murders—no evidence, no leads, no time to waste —but Stitch keeps dragging her into dangerous territory, and she has no idea how close the killer is to making her his final victim.

As the killer's obsession with Susan escalates, Stitch realizes his criminal past might be exactly what she needs to survive. Because sometimes the only way to protect what you love is to embrace the darkness inside.

Get ready for sizzling chemistry, heart-stopping suspense, and a bad boy who'll risk everything—including his freedom—to save the woman who owns his soul.

For Newman & Amelia's Story
Finding Redemption
A Slaying Love Novel, #5

A disgraced ex-detective. A woman who won't give up. A case that could save them both.

Ex-Detective Newman wants to be left alone to wallow in the wreckage of his ruined career and shattered life. When a gorgeous woman with vibrant pink hair and a stubborn streak shows up at his door, he wants nothing to do with her case—or the way she makes him feel like he might be worth saving.

Amelia Benedict doesn't take no for an answer, especially when her younger brother's life hangs in the balance. The police think he ran away, but she knows something terrible has happened. A disgraced ex-cop with nothing left to lose and everything to prove, Newman definitely isn't the right guy for the case—but he's her last hope. But as they dig deeper into her brother's disappearance, they uncover a web of danger that threatens to destroy what's left of Newman's soul and put Amelia in the crosshairs of a killer.

In a race against time to save an innocent boy, Newman must decide if redemption is worth the risk—because this time, failure doesn't just mean losing his last chance at salvation. It means losing the woman who believed in him when no one else would.

Get ready for second-chance redemption, heart-stopping suspense, & a broken hero who'll risk everything to prove he's worth loving.

ABOUT THE AUTHOR

I'm a *USA Today* Bestselling Author that loves to write contemporary romance and romantic suspense novels, although I am partial to romantic suspense. I even dabble in paranormal. Honestly, I love anything that has to do with romance. As long as there's a happy ending, I'm a happy camper. And insta-love...yes, please! I love baseball (Go Twins!) and creating awesome crafts. I graduated with a Bachelor's Degree in Criminal Justice, working in that field for several years before I became a stay-at-home mom. I have a few more amazing stories in the works. If you would like to learn more about me and my books, head to my website by scanning the QR code. Thanks for reading!

Scan me

www.ingramcontent.com/pod-product-compliance
Lightning Source LLC
Chambersburg PA
CBHW020843260626
47169CB00003B/1107